leap of faith

JAMIE BLAIR

SIMON & SCHUSTER BFYR

New York London Toronto Sydney New Delhi

An imprint of Simon & Schuster Children's Publishing Division
1230 Avenue of the Americas, New York, New York 10020
For information about special discounts for bulk purchases, please contact Simon & Schuster Special Sales at 1-866-506-1949 or business@simonandschuster.com.
The Simon & Schuster Speakers Bureau can bring authors to your live event. For more information or to book an event, contact the Simon & Schuster Speakers Bureau at 1-866-248-3049 or visit our website at www.simonspeakers.com.
Also available in a SIMON & SCHUSTER BFYR hardcover edition
Book design by Krista Vossen
Cover photographs (left to right) copyright © 2013 by JonPaul Douglass/Flickr/ Getty Images, Fotosearch/Getty Images, Klaus Vedfelt/Riser/Getty Images; cover composite by Shasti O'Leary Soudant copyright © 2013 by Simon & Schuster, Inc.
The text for this book is set in Sabon LT Std.
First SIMON & SCHUSTER BFYR paperback edition September 2014
2 4 6 8 10 9 7 5 3 1
The Library of Congress has cataloged the hardcover edition as follows:
Blair, Jamie M.
Leap of Faith / Jamie Blair. — 1st. ed.
p. cm
Summary: Seventeen-year-old Faith shepherds her neglectful, drug-addicted mother through her pregnancy and then kidnaps the baby, taking on the responsibility of being her baby sister's parent while hiding from the authorities.
ISBN 978-1-4424-4713-4 (hardcover)
ISBN 978-1-4424-4715-8 (eBook)
[1. Kidnapping—Fiction. 2. Runaways—Fiction. 3. Fugitives from justice—Fiction. 4. Parenting—Fiction.] I. Title.
PZ7.B53783Le 2013
[Fic]—dc23
2012043125
ISBN 978-1-4424-4716-5 (pbk)

To mothers and sisters
and the special bond we share

chapter

one

The bangbangbanging of Mom's headboard against my wall needs to stop before my head explodes. I'm exhausted and wish he'd just leave so I can sleep. Of course Mom's bed has to be shoved right up against the other side of my wall.

I roll my eyes and take a deep breath, pulling the covers up higher around my neck. After a few minutes, her door creaks open and he comes out shirtless, his stained T-shirt dangling from his fingers. She's wearing a dingy terry-cloth robe around her skeleton-thin body. I squeeze my eyes closed and roll over, trying to block out the sound of their voices.

Disgusting. I'll be shocked if I ever have a normal sex life. My ex, Jason, says she's scarring me in some kind of sexually repressive way. He's probably right. I'll be a virgin forever.

Sex isn't dirty, Faith, he whispered on our last night together while trying to slide my jeans down over my hips.

You're not your mom, and I'm not some random guy. I love you.

Didn't matter.

I wouldn't do it.

The chain on the front door slides, then rattles against the wood frame as it dangles and the door is tugged open.

"Bye, hon," Mom says. I hear her lighter flick to life. Her voice is raspy from everything she smokes. "Cross your fingers." She laughs, and I picture his sausage-size fingers crossed. His feet must be back in his boots, because they tromp out onto the stoop. "Tell Angel hi for me, and have her cross her fingers too!"

The door closes, and she lets out a whoop of excitement. "Faith, honey, you asleep?" Her bare feet patter to my bedroom door, and she snaps on the light.

I flip over and glare at her. "Oddly enough, no."

She rubs a thin stack of twenties between her thumb and finger. In the dark hallway, the cherry at the end of her Marlboro Light glows in her other hand. "It's a shame Dave and I had to try again. Knocking me up is getting expensive for him." She laughs and fans herself with the cash. She's three weeks pregnant but is milking him for all the money she can before telling him.

He might be drug-dealing scum, but he and his girlfriend, Angel, don't deserve to be lied to. They just want a baby. They couldn't have picked a worse person to be their egg donor-baby carrier, but Mom comes cheap—well, cheaper than the traditional route. Mom will do anything for money.

Throwing my blanket back, I shove off from my mattress on the floor and stand up. The worn, shit brown carpet feels gummy under my bare toes as I walk toward her. "Give me that." My hand darts for her smoke.

"Don't be stupid. My mother smoked with me. I smoked with you." She throws her hand behind her back, out of my reach. Her hair's matted and sticks out in all directions. It reminds me of a dog's butt after it scoots across the carpet.

I tilt my head and sneer at her. "It's not your baby this time. Let's try to keep it alive, shall we?"

"Christ, Faith. Can't you just enjoy the moment with me?" She waves the stack of bills in my face.

"Why?" I push past her. "It's not mine."

She follows me through the living room, into the kitchen. "No shit it's not yours. You're not the one who's going to be as big as a barn in a few months, have to push this thing out and be left with stretch marks all over your ass. I deserve to be paid for suffering through this, don't I?"

I bend and stick my head in the fridge. "You chose to do it."

She grabs my arm and yanks me up. Her lips are drawn tight and quiver with anger. "You don't pay the electric bill. You don't put food in the fridge."

I laugh, knowing it'll piss her off. "You don't put food in the fridge either. Never have. Who do you think you're kidding? Hope and I had ketchup packets for dinner some nights when we were little. . . ."

Her blue eyes flame. She clenches her jaw so tightly, her dyed red hair shakes. Her hands grip the belt of her bathrobe, and she yanks it tighter. "Find yourself somewhere else to live. I'm done being your mother. You're nothing but a bitch and have been since the day you were born."

"Done being my mother? That's funny." I roll my eyes. "I didn't know you ever started." She tells me to get the hell out all the time. She'd be screwed if I ever really left—less cash from Uncle Sam for her dependent minors.

I turn back to the fridge while she stalks out of the kitchen and into the living room, fishes her cigarettes out of her pocket, then lights another.

Her anger cuts a smile into my face. I slam the refrigerator door and stride into the living room for round two. "Give me that cigarette!" I snag it from her fingers, burning my palm in the process. "Shit!" The cigarette falls to the carpet.

Mom swoops down and snatches it up. "I hope it hurts like hell. The carpet's singed." She shoves me, but I don't budge. She's not strong enough to hurt me physically, and she knows it.

I laugh at her again. "I'm going to have the best nine months of my life keeping you from smokes, pills, booze, weed—all the things you love."

The only time I remember my mom sober was when she did it for Frank. Frank was a trucker she met when I was eleven. She was a waitress at the all-night truck stop down by the highway exit. Frank had been sober for ten years and wouldn't date a junkie. Mom went to rehab. For him. Not for me and Hope.

We had our first and only family vacation ever—plus Frank—in Florida. Under my mattress I still have a picture of me, Mom, and Hope standing in the surf. When Mom's trashed, or being Bitch from Hell, sometimes I pull it out and go back to my Happy Place beside the ocean. I try to hear waves instead of her headboard.

Mom was sober for three months, then she met Dave. Frank left and never came back, and so did Mom's sobriety. She's such a trashy loser.

The front door squeaks as Hope pushes it open. "Is it over?" She comes inside and looks back and forth between Mom and me.

"Yeah, you missed quite a performance tonight too," I say, and plod back to me and Hope's room.

"Thank God." Hope walks past Mom and follows me.

I lie back down on my mattress and pull the blanket over my shoulders. Hope kicks off her running shoes and tugs the elastic band out of her golden blond hair. I've always wanted her hair. Mine's the dirty beige of my mom's roots when they grow out. Hope has beautiful blue eyes too, and I'm stuck with the same shit brown color of our carpet.

Maybe if we'd had the same dad, we'd look more alike.

Tomorrow's the first day of school, Hope's first day of her senior year. She'll be graduating a couple months after Mom gives birth to Dave's demon spawn.

Hope will leave.

The baby will leave.

It'll just be Mom and me for another year.

I have to get out.

Hope strips off her sweaty running clothes and heads out of our bedroom in her underwear. "Jumping in the shower."

"Whatever. Turn the light off."

The thought of Hope moving out makes me nauseous. It's always been the two of us against Mom. Hope joined the track team in eighth grade and hasn't stopped running since. It's not just an immediate way to get the hell out of the house but an escape from this shit life altogether. She has a scholarship to Ohio State. She'll leave and never look back.

I'm not so fortunate. My grades kind of suck. I'm not athletic, since Mom smoked when she was pregnant with me, giving me the lifelong gift of asthma, and I'll need to get student loans if I want to go to college. If there's a college that will even accept me with a D average. Working five nights a week in a pizza parlor for the perk of free food doesn't leave a lot of time for studying.

I roll over and face the wall. My stomach growls. I

should've eaten at work. I glance up at the red and white cardboard Leaning Tower of Pisa that I cut out from a pizza box and taped to my wall. I make pizzas at Giovanni's at night and on weekends. Pepperoni grease clings to everything and makes my hair slick and my face break out. That's the only downfall, though. I've worked there for a year now. I'd love to have my own pizza place someday. But that'll never happen, because *this* is my shitty life. I won't fool myself into thinking it could ever be more.

The shower blasts on in the bathroom, making the pipes bang. We get three minutes' worth of hot water, so we shower fast.

I hear mom shuffle into her bedroom and shut the door. The dragon's in its den for the night.

I think again about harassing the hell out of her for the next nine months and snicker to myself. This is going to be the best revenge ever. She'll be miserable, and I'll be the one making her that way. I feel like laughing diabolically and drumming my fingers together.

Hope opens the door, and a waft of steam floats into our room. I roll back over as she comes in. In the dark, I only see a shadow of her arm rising and tugging a comb through her hair. She plops down on her mattress. Hope has a box spring too. Guess I'll inherit that when she leaves. It doesn't make me feel any better about it, though.

"How was your run?"

Her shoulders rise and fall. "Fine."

"Is Brian in any of your classes this year?" Brian and Hope have dated since they were freshmen. They plan to get married. He's going to OSU after graduation too, to play football. She spends more time at his house than she does at home.

I need a boyfriend. I used to spend a lot of time at Jason's before he dumped me. I should've just screwed him. At least I'd still have somewhere to go.

"A couple." She sounds down.

"What's wrong?"

She sighs. "Just . . . I don't know. Did Mom tell Dave she's pregnant yet?"

I snort. "What do you think?"

She throws herself back on her bed. "I can't believe she's doing this. I mean, it's low even for her."

"Yeah." *And I'll be stuck here another year.* "Don't worry. I plan to make her suffer through this pregnancy. She'll take care of this baby whether she wants to or not. First thing tomorrow, I'm flushing all her pot. A new school year, and a fresh start."

"She's going to kill you." Hope scoots under her blanket.

"I can't wait to see her try."

"You have issues." She yawns.

I laugh. "So do you."

I empty the three baggies I found into the toilet and press the corroded handle. The water lurches into a spin, taking the weed spiraling down, down, down. Then it's gone.

Hope walks by the bathroom with her backpack. "I can't believe you really did it. Seriously, she's going to kill you."

I shrug and turn back to the empty toilet bowl. "She won't be awake for hours. I'll be at school, and then work."

She walks into the living room, her golden hair trailing down her back. "You have to come home sometime. Hey, Brian's here. You riding with us?" I hear her yank the front door open.

"Yeah, I'll grab my stuff."

When I get outside to Brian's car, they're staring at each

other with googly eyes. I want to puke. His big football-grabbing hand is wrapped around her thigh. Her hand's on his cheek. Hope has no issues with sex. That's something else she managed to escape.

I open the back door of the Honda coupe and slide in after my backpack. "Please stop groping until I'm out of the car, 'kay? Thanks."

Brian laughs and looks over his shoulder at me. "What's up, Faith? How's work?"

Brian and I have zero to talk about, but I have to give him props for trying. "Good. How's football?"

For the next fifteen minutes, until we pull into North High School's parking lot, Brian fills me in on every detail of their summer practices, and how they're going to kick Central's asses all over the field next Friday night—the first game of the season.

I know Hope's heard all of it already, probably more than once, but she listens, riveted. God, that has to be love, because I'm bored out of my skull and want to kick my own ass for asking him about football.

After we park, I lug my bag out of Brian's car and wave. "See ya."

"Need a ride home?" Brian asks, closing his car door.

"No. Thanks for asking, though."

Hope darts out of the car and grabs my arm. "I have track after school, and then Brian and I are eating at his house. I won't be home until late." She bites the inside of her cheek.

"Don't worry. Mom isn't going to actually *kill* me, you know." I pat her on the head like a little kid and chuckle. "See ya tonight."

Even though I try to appear like it doesn't bother me, like I'm not terrified of Mom's wrath, my insides are a twisted knot. I shouldn't have flushed her weed. She loves it more than she loves me. It's possible that she *will* kill me.

It takes until lunch. A student assistant finds me in the back corner of the lunchroom. "Your mom's in the office," she says.

My stomach lurches, threatening to heave up the chocolate Ho Hos I just ate.

"Shit."

chapter

two

I can't breathe. Maybe my lungs have collapsed. It feels like my chest is pressed flat against my back. I'm light-headed as I follow the student assistant through the office door.

Mom's leaning against the counter with her back to me, wearing beat-up jeans and a paint-splattered blue sweatshirt. She turns when the door closes. Her sunken, black-ringed eyes drill into me. I try not to cringe. "We almost forgot your doctor's appointment," she says.

She's going to make me leave with her. I blurt the first thing that comes to mind. "Maybe we should reschedule it. I have a test in algebra today."

"Today is your first day. You have a test already?" Her eyebrows shoot skyward.

Dumb—that was dumb to say. "It's, like, a skills test. To see how much we know already."

"Well, then, you're fine. Everyone knows you don't know shit."

The secretary gasps and swivels her chair, not wanting any part of our conversation.

This is why I don't have friends.

I know how much my life sucks.

I don't need to see it in another person's appalled expression.

I can't imagine why Hope would subject herself to that, but whatever.

I sigh. "Let me get my bag. I'll meet you at the car."

I'm so fucking dead, I'm so fucking dead, I chant in my head all the way to my locker on the second floor. Why must I do stupid shit that I regret later? It's like I can't get in deep enough and have to keep digging myself down into a hole. Then I stand at the bottom, look up, and realize I'm fucked and have no way back out.

My fingers twist the locker combination, and I frantically brainstorm a way out of this. The only thing I can do is work the baby angle. Pretend I actually give a shit about the future tweaker she's carrying.

Play it up.

Maybe even cry a little.

It's my only shot.

I shove the school doors open and shuffle out into the parking lot, momentarily blinded by the sun. My feet move forward with resolve. I can do this. She can't be mad at me for protecting the kid, right? I mean, she doesn't get the big cash until she actually has it. I'm just looking out for her best interest. *Yes*—there's the angle.

I nod to myself, believing the line of bull surging through my mind. Her fifteen-year-old black and rusty Oldsmobile pulls up beside me, almost running over my foot, and lunges to a halt. My teeth grind together, and a pang of anxiety squeezes through my chest as I reach for the handle and open the car door.

She's screaming before my ass hits the seat.

"Who the *fuck* do you think you are? You didn't pay for that! You owe me two hundred bucks!"

Her foot slams the gas pedal. My head hits the back of the seat, and I struggle with the seat belt. "Okay. I was just looking out for the baby. And you. I mean, you don't get paid until it's born, right? What if it comes out with two heads or something? You want your money, don't you?"

"You weren't looking out for the baby or me. You were being an asshole. That's what you are, Faith, an asshole." Her hand pounds the steering wheel to punctuate her point.

"Seriously, Mom, you have to keep that kid safe. You want the cash, right?" I dig my fingernails into my palm, trying to make my eyes water. "I don't want anything to happen to the baby," I say in a choked-up voice. "Please, Mom, think of the baby."

Her foot lets up on the gas, and her head slowly turns in my direction. Her eyes focus on mine, like she's seeing me for the first time ever. "Who the hell *are* you? You never cry. What's all this baby bullshit anyway? You know it's not ours, right? Don't go getting attached to it."

I roll my eyes. "*Puh-lease.* These are tears of joy for getting to give you shit for forty weeks." I yank my sleeve down over my hand and wipe at my eyes.

She snaps her head back toward the window. "You do know that I'm the mom, right? No matter what you might think of my parenting skills."

I choke again, fighting back a laugh.

"You have no say in anything relating to me or this ten-thousand-dollar kid inside me."

"Right." For the first time, I look around us. "Where are we going?"

"The bank. You're taking out two hundred bucks to pay me back for the weed you flushed."

I burst out laughing. "Seriously? You think I'm paying you back so you can go buy more? Not a chance."

Her arm shoots out like lightning. The back of her hand connects with my mouth. "You want to be a smart-ass? Huh? Keep it up, and I'll knock every tooth you have right out of your head!"

The salty taste of warm blood fills my mouth. I probe around with my tongue until a searing pain shoots through my lip where my top tooth made a gash.

She pulls up to the ATM, rolls down her window, and holds out her hand. "Give me your card."

Everything inside me clenches in anger. My fingers rip the zipper on my backpack open and yank out my wallet. I shove the card into her hand without looking at her and recite the pin. "Four seven six five."

My lip throbs as she punches the numbers into the keypad. A minute later, I hear the whirr of the machine spitting out cash.

My cash.

My meager means of escaping.

I hate her.

I hate her with an all-encompassing passion that I thrive on more than food. I *will* make her sorry.

She stuffs my money and my bank card into her purse and puts the car in drive.

I want my card, but I don't want her to backhand me again. It sets off a tug-of-war in my brain. She knows I want to ask for it. By not asking, I'm making her think I'm afraid of her.

I'm not afraid of her.

"I want my card back." I suck my lip in, preparing for another blow.

Instead, she laughs. "I'm keeping it in case you pull another stunt like you did this morning. Next time I won't have to come haul your ass out of school and waste my gas. I'll just go right to the bank." Her eyebrows shoot up as she smiles at me, a *How do you like that?* smile.

I don't like it.

But she's a drunk and a junkie. She'll get baked, and I'll take my card back. No big deal.

She lights a cigarette, cracks the window, and runs her long fingernails through her hair. At the next street, she makes a right. "Gotta make a stop," she says.

Of course we do. All those twenties are burning a hole through her purse.

The car lurches to a stop in front of a run-down duplex with a saggy roof. "Stay here," she says.

I watch her stick-figure frame head up the walkway and onto the porch. Dave—Baby Daddy—answers the door and lets her inside.

Ten minutes go by and a car as rusty and beat as my mom's pulls into the driveway. A woman with long black hair gets out and carries two plastic grocery bags across the bare dirt yard and takes them into Dave's place. It must be his girl-friend, Angel—Baby Mama.

I try to picture a red and white tricycle on the sidewalk and struggle to form the image in my mind. It's just not right. This isn't a swing-set-and-baby-pool kind of place. The entire neighborhood is a drug-infested hole.

No kid can grow up here.

Mom comes out pinching the bridge of her nose and shoving baggies into her purse. She sniffs and snuffles all the way home. When we get inside, she cracks open a can of beer and throws herself onto the couch.

In my room, I toss my backpack on my bed and hear the TV come on. The clock reads ten till two. I should be in school for another twenty-five minutes. I don't have to be at work until five. Three hours to kill, wanting to be anywhere but here.

I should've just screwed Jason. He would've picked me up. He's twenty-two and has his own place. Hell, I could probably live with him. Mom doesn't give a shit.

For a minute, I contemplate calling him and telling him I want to have sex with him. I wonder if he'd even be interested, if he'd come get me, since we've been apart for six months. I doubt he'd believe I'd suddenly be willing to give up my virginity to him. He's tried enough times to know I won't do it. He may be a low-life pizza delivery guy with no ambition, but he's not dumb.

I lie on my mattress and stare out the window, up into the trees. I hate my life. I want out of it so bad, sometimes I think I might die.

My thoughts wander back to Baby Daddy's apartment with the dirt yard, peeling paint, and hookers at the end of the street—and my mom coming out after snorting something and buying more weed.

A baby can't live there. Its life would suck more than mine.

chapter

three

I come home from work to find Mom's bedroom door closed. The murmur of a male voice tells me she's not alone.

She has more than just a small baby bump now, and some guy is in there—ugh, the thought of it repulses me.

I turn the TV up louder to drown out their voices. "Happy fucking New Year to me."

The ball drops, and I have another shitty year to look forward to. Hope leaves home this year. The baby's born this year and is taken away, along with my excuse for harassing my mom to stop doing drugs.

I flip open the pizza box that I brought home from work and grab a slice. The cheese is hot and stringy and oozes down the sides onto my fingers.

Just as I'm about to take my first bite, there's a knock at the door. I toss my slice back into the box, wipe my hands on my jeans, and make my way across the room to the door. I tug it open, and a woman with long, dark hair is standing there.

"Is Dave here?" she asks.

Baby Mama. I thought she looked familiar. "No."

She narrows her eyes. "His truck just appeared on the street outside your house?"

I stick my head out the door. Damn, she's right. His truck is out there. "Oh. I just got home from work a little while ago. Guess he is here." Banging my mom.

"Tell him to get his ass home, okay? I've got a house full of people with money wanting to party."

I nod. "Sure."

She looks like she's about to say something else but spins around and jogs down the steps. I watch her get into her rust-bucket car and back out of the driveway, hitting every rut along the way.

"Who was that?"

I jump about ten feet into the air at Mom's voice behind me. "You scared the hell out of me!" I turn and lean into the door. My butt pushes it closed. She's outside her bedroom in her skanky pink bathrobe with Dave beside her smoothing his greasy hair. "Dave's woman. She wants his ass home. Something about people partying and money . . . I don't know."

Both of their faces fall.

"How did she know you were here?" Mom asks him, pushing up her sleeve and rubbing her fingers over the tracks on her arm.

He shakes his head. "Shit." He yanks his T-shirt on and pulls his brown work boots onto his feet. "I'll call you." He dashes out the door and slams it behind him.

"Whatever." Mom runs her fingers through the back of her hair, where its typical, postsex, matted, Irish-Setter-butt style is happening.

I sit back on the couch and pick up my pizza again. "Tell me he's not dumb enough to believe you suddenly gained ten pounds in just your gut. He does know you're pregnant, right?"

She smirks. "Of course he knows."

"So . . ." I raise my eyebrows.

"We were just having fun, okay? God. I don't know why I'd expect you to know anything about that. Here you are, New Year's Eve, sitting home alone eating pizza on Mommy's couch."

"My life's not exactly conducive to relationships."

"Hope's is. She has no problem with friends and a boyfriend. Looks like it's just you, sweetie. You're the one who's got the problem." She stalks into the bathroom and closes the door. The shower comes on and the pipes start banging.

A week into the new year, I'm sitting in the obstetrician's office with Mom. I called and made the appointment and threatened to tell Angel that she was screwing Dave if she didn't come.

"Ms. Kurtz," the doctor says after Mom's exam, "at or around twenty weeks, we do an ultrasound to make sure the baby's developing. After you're dressed, a nurse will be in to take you to the ultrasound room." The doctor hands Mom a couple of packets of prenatal vitamins, makes a few notes in Mom's chart, and leaves the room.

Mom slides off the examination table. The paper gown rustles as she moves. "You're paying for the ultrasound. I'm not wasting my money on that. It's your fault I'm even here." She tosses the vitamins onto my lap. "And I'm not taking these."

My eyes roll. "I'm sure Dave will pay for an ultrasound of his child." I tuck the vitamins into her purse. "Are you going to find out what it is?"

Her eyebrows lower as she fastens her bra. "It's a baby, Faith. I thought you knew that already."

"A girl or a boy—hello?"

She shrugs. "Who cares? All I care about is this whole thing being halfway over. Eighteen more weeks until I'm ten grand richer."

The nurse knocks and pokes her head in just as Mom finishes getting dressed. "All set?" she asks.

"As set as I'll ever be." Mom snatches her purse from my lap and follows the nurse out of the room.

Down the hall to the right, the nurse gets Mom situated on another table and pulls the waist of her pants down below her belly.

"This will be warm," the nurse says, and squirts some clear jelly on Mom's stomach. "You can come in," she says to me, motioning me in from the doorway. "Are you hoping for a brother or a sister?"

I take a few steps farther into the room as the nurse presses the probe to Mom's stomach and the screen comes to life with a black-and-white image of a tiny, moving baby. "Either's fine."

Transfixed, I stare at the screen in awe. It's actually a baby, not a blob or a clump of cells, but a baby with arms, legs, everything. Its little hands wave around like it's swimming. Tiny feet kick.

The nurse takes pictures and measurements. Mom has her eyes closed. It looks like she's sleeping.

"Do you want to know the sex?" the nurse asks.

"I do," I say. "I want to know."

The nurse looks to Mom, who makes a grunting noise. "Sure. Whatever."

I can't take my eyes from the screen. The nurse maneuvers

the ultrasound wand to try to get a look between the baby's legs. The baby squirms, making it difficult.

Finally, the nurse says, "There. It's a girl."

"A girl," I whisper. She's beautiful. I can already tell she looks a little bit like Hope.

"Okay," the nurse says, and takes the wand off Mom's stomach. "We're all done." She gives Mom some tissues to wipe the slime off her belly.

"About time," Mom says, yanking up her pants. "Let's go, Faith. You should be satisfied now." She throws her purse over her shoulder and leaves the room.

"Thanks," I tell the nurse.

She turns on her stool and holds out black-and-white photos for me to take. "Don't forget these." Her forehead's creased. She's concerned. For me. Or the baby. I'm not sure. Maybe both.

I take the photos and stuff them into my pocket. "Thank you."

"I don't think she looks like me," Hope says, holding the ultrasound pictures over her head, toward the light.

We're lying on our beds. I'm trying to figure out how to bribe Mom to take the prenatal vitamins. Maybe I can dissolve the vitamins in coffee.

"Why do you have these, anyway?" Hope tosses the pictures toward my bed. I catch two, but the third falls to the floor.

"'Cuz the nurse handed them to me. Mom doesn't want them." I stretch my arm out, reach the picture on the floor with my fingertip, and slide it over to myself.

"Why do you?" She hoists one leg in the air and reaches for her toes, stretching.

I shrug. "I don't."

"You kept them." She switches legs.

"You can't just throw something like that away. I'll give them to Dave next time he comes over to bang Mom."

"Eww. Don't say that. You know I can't stand to think about her and men . . . right in there." She points toward Mom's room with her toes. "Four and a half more months and I'm out of here."

I sigh and roll to my side, facing her. "Don't remind me."

She lowers her leg. "You'll be fine. It's not like I'm here all that much now."

"No, but I know you'll be back every night. I'm not alone in this hell."

She laughs. "So, it's a case of misery loves company, is that it? You don't want to suffer alone?"

The corners of my mouth turn up. "Maybe."

"I'll sneak you into my dorm room overnight a few times this summer, okay?"

"Gee, thanks." I roll my eyes. "You're a lifesaver."

She gets up and flips off the light. "It's all I can do. I'm sorry. You know you have to find a way out of here, right? I don't know how I'm going to get through even one semester without worrying about you."

I dig my feet under my blanket and pull it up to my shoulders. "I know. I'll think of something. Don't worry."

"I'll always worry. I love you, Faithy."

"Love you too."

In the morning, I make a pot of coffee, dissolve two prenatal vitamins in it, and leave a note, pretending to be a wonderful, thoughtful daughter who just happened to make her mom coffee before she left for school.

She'll know something's up, but I don't think she'll know what. She'll drink it.

I ride with Brian and Hope again, staring out the window in the backseat, listening to them make plans for the weekend. Again, I'm nagged by the urge to call Jason. All I do is work and go to school. I need more in my life, and not just because I want to have somewhere else to go besides home.

Strands of Hope's golden hair glint in the winter sunlight streaming through the windshield. A pang of sadness reverberates through me. I don't want her to go. I hate that she's eighteen, graduating, and moving out. I hate that the track team starts practice over the summer and she has to be there the third week of June. I hate that she's brave enough to go out and live her life.

I wish I was brave.

chapter

four

The car's trunk is about to burst, and so is Mom's stomach. The doctor put her on bed rest, and she's pissed. Now that she can't drive and has no reason to deny me using the car, I've spent most of spring break driving around to get away from her.

"Do you need help with that?" the woman asks. I'm at a yard sale and bought a stroller for the baby.

"No, I'll get it in here." I shove a car seat and a Pack 'n Play to the far sides of Mom's trunk and jiggle the stroller in between. "There. Got it."

"Hope your baby likes it!" she calls, and waves over her shoulder, walking back up the driveway.

"I'm sure she will." I get in the car and turn the key in the ignition. I don't think about what I've been doing all spring break, hitting yard sale after yard sale, collecting baby items. I just do it. I haven't let myself admit why, though. That would be admitting I'm fucking crazy, and really, I don't know that yet, because I don't have a plan, because I won't let myself think of one.

It's this circular thought process that's gotten me through the last week.

The one thing I do know is that this baby isn't going to live the fucked-up life I've had for the past sixteen years. In the past few months, I've memorized those ultrasound pictures down to the last detail and driven past Dave and Angel's place probably a hundred times.

I've seen drugged-up partiers passed out on their porch. I've seen the cops parked outside twice. I've seen enough drug dealers and whores for a lifetime. My little sister *will not* live there.

Not to mention, Dave's still screwing my mom.

I've seen Angel's own "visitor" come by their duplex late at night when Dave's at my house. Those two don't want a baby. They don't even want each other. It's obvious they were high when they made the decision to bring my mom into their effed-up plan.

My knuckles had gone pale, I'm gripping the steering wheel so tight. This baby is weighing heavy on my mind. I can't ignore it.

Hope said I have to find my own way out.

I've found it.

I just can't think about it.

Because that would be admitting I'm fucking crazy.

And the circle of thought continues all the way home until I'm inside and faced with my mom—out of bed and stoned on the couch with a can of beer in her hand.

Before she can say a word, I stride into my bedroom and close the door. It's best to avoid her when she's trashed. She likes to pick fights.

I lie down and close my eyes. My room is blessedly pitch black. It's been warm for late April, and the crickets are loud outside my window, but they're lulling me to sleep. It's that time right before you pass out when you're not sure if you're dreaming or still awake. That's why Mom's voice doesn't seem real at first.

"FAITH!"

"Huh?" I sit up and rub my blurry eyes.

"Faith, for Christ's sake—get in here and help me!"

I stand and trip over my blanket, which is tangled around my feet. "I'm coming!"

She wails and I dart across the hall, dragging the blanket and tripping into the living room, where she's still sprawled on the couch. "What's wrong? Are you okay?"

She pushes on the back of the couch, trying to get up. "Well, help me! Shit, Faith, what good are you?" Then she cries out again.

"Holy shit! You're in labor!" She's two weeks early. I grab her hand and try to tug her up. She grimaces in pain. I wish Hope were here. She's much better at dealing with Mom. "I'll call Brian's house and tell Hope to come home."

"Just get me in the car!" I grip her hand with both of mine and pull her to her feet. "Ahhh!" she shrieks.

"Okay. It's okay. Breathe." I wrap an arm around her back.

"Shut the fuck up, Faith! Just get me to the hospital."

Fighting the urge to throw her to the floor and go back to bed, I grab her packed bag from her bedroom and help her out to the car.

She screams, cries, and cusses all the way to the hospital. I drive fast, actually hoping I'll get pulled over and the cop can drag her butt to the maternity ward.

I pull up in front of the emergency room doors and hop

out, flagging down an orderly with a wheelchair. "My mom's in labor!"

It all happens really fast. Before I know it, she's in a gown, hooked up to monitors, and almost ten centimeters dilated.

I don't know if Dave and Angel want to be there for the delivery or not, and I don't want to ask. Instead I say, "Should I call Hope?"

"For what?" Mom says, relaxed now from her epidural. "We aren't keeping this baby. It'll all be over soon."

I nod. "I know. Just thought I'd ask." She doesn't mention Angel and Dave.

The doctor and a nurse come in to check her and say it's time to push. "Are you staying?" the doctor asks me.

I shrug. "I guess."

The doctor smiles. "It'll be a good learning experience for you."

Yeah. Contraception 101. Not that I'll ever let a guy devirginize me. Especially not now that they've got Mom's legs hoisted up and she's baring all. Not a chance. I'll never be in that situation.

"Come stand by me," the doctor says, motioning me over.

"I don't want to look." I can feel the repulsed expression on my face.

"It's a baby. There's nothing gross about it."

I have no interest in seeing my mom "down there," but I inch a little closer so the doctor will leave me alone.

"Okay," she says to my mom, "on three you're going to—"

"I know how to do this!" Mom snaps. "I've had two already!"

"One. Two. Three. Push!"

Mom crunches practically in half and groans as she pushes. Her face turns red, then purple as the doctor counts to ten.

"Good," the doctor says. "The next contraction should be coming . . . right . . . now! Push!"

Mom bears down again. Her face turns red, then purple while the doctor counts to ten. This routine continues for forty minutes. A second nurse comes in pushing a baby scale.

"Her head's right here," the doctor says. "Come see," she says to me.

Oh, God. I don't want to look. But she won't stop crooking her finger at me. The look on her face is so intent and excited, I take a few steps closer and peer over the doctor's shoulder.

"See her hair?" The doctor rubs the top of the baby's head with her finger, ruffling the wet, dark, feather-fine hair.

My mouth is open, gaping at the baby's head. She's right there, ready to come out and be a person in the world. It's actually kind of awesome.

The doctor tells Mom to push again. Three more times, and the baby's whole head and shoulders emerge. On the fourth push, the doctor pulls the baby free.

The nurses start rushing around, swabbing the baby's mouth, wiping the white goo from her face.

The baby starts screaming at the top of her lungs and flailing around.

"Want to cut the cord?" the doctor asks me, shoving a pair of surgical scissors into my hand.

"Uh . . . okay."

She shows me where to cut, and I squeeze the scissors around the cord. It's hard, like cutting through rubber.

Once I cut the baby free from my mom, they clean her, weigh her, wrap her in a pink, white, and blue blanket, and tug a matching knit hat onto her head.

The nurse hands her to me and announces, "Six pounds,

four ounces, and twenty inches." She glances over to my unin-
terested mother, then back at me. "Does she have a name?"

I look down at the baby in my arms. Dark blue eyes. Brown
fuzzy hair. Red, puffy cheeks. "Addy," I whisper.

Once you name it, it's yours.

Someone said that once.

I don't remember who, but it's true. I named her. She's
mine.

The next day at two o'clock, they release Mom and Addy, since
Mom doesn't have insurance. I went home last night while
Mom was sleeping and packed a duffel bag full of everything
I own, which isn't much. This morning, I took a shower and
told Hope that I love her. She was in a shitty mood and just
said, "Whatever, Faith. You're so strange sometimes."

An orderly comes into Mom's hospital room with a wheelchair, which pisses Mom off because she can walk to the car
on her own. She wants to know how much she'll be charged
for the dumbass who pushes the wheelchair.

The plan is for Dave and Angel to come over as soon as we
get home with the baby and take her.

Too bad for them.

She'll never get there.

I carry Addy, all bundled in her blanket, down the hall
to the elevator. The man pushing Mom follows. We all ride
down to the ground level together.

"I'll go get the baby buckled into her car seat and pull the
car up out front," I say.

Mom's digging through her purse on her lap distractedly.
"Mm-hmm. I can't find my cigarettes."

I leave her there, searching through her purse and completely unaware that I've found my escape.

Addy's face scrunches up in the sunlight. I hold her closer and jog across the street to the parking garage. Mom's keys poke against my thigh.

I got to the hospital early enough to get a spot on the bottom level of the deck. I open the driver's-side door, pull the seat release, and lean into the backseat, where I've secured the car seat.

Addy's sound asleep by the time I've lowered her into her rear-facing seat and buckled her into the five-point harness.

"Ready to start your life, little one?" I run my finger along the side of her cheek. It's the softest thing I've ever felt. "Your big sister will figure out what to do. Don't worry." My heart drums a fast rhythm under my skin. I can't fail us.

I buckle myself in, turn the key, and press down on the accelerator. As I pull out of the garage, I look across the street to the hospital entrance. Mom's sitting outside in the wheelchair smoking, totally oblivious to the fact that I've just taken her ten-thousand-dollar golden goose.

chapter

five

I'm sick to my stomach and scared as hell. My eyes dart to the rearview mirror every five seconds to see if I'm being chased down by the cops. I screwed Mom over royally. She's going to kill me this time for sure.

I'm so fucking dead. *I'm so fucking dead!*

Addy wakes up and shrieks.

"Don't cry, baby, we're like Thelma and Louise! Two crazy women—wild and free!"

She cries a few more minutes, then it fades to a whimper and goes silent. I know I'll have to pull over every three hours or so to give her a bottle and change her diaper. All the supplies I need are in the trunk—bottles, formula, diapers, wipes, rash cream, clothes, pacifiers—one of everything in Walmart's baby aisle.

The map in the glove box was marked with my route to Florida three days ago when I finally gave in to my plan. I don't even need to look at it. I know it by heart. All I need is a clue about what to do when we get there.

Money won't be a problem for a little while. This morning, I emptied five hundred dollars out of my account and also took all the money left from the stash in Mom's dresser drawer that Dave gave her when he was trying to knock her up—almost a thousand dollars.

It should get us a cheap motel room for a couple of nights, until I find something permanent. Of course, I'll need more diapers and formula for Addy, and food for me.

I'll need a job.

And a babysitter.

My head starts to spin. I can't think about all of this right now. Now is the time to drive. Everything else will fall into place later. It has to.

Around five o'clock, Addy starts crying. We still haven't left Ohio, almost to the West Virginia border. I pull into a rest area, pop the trunk, and hop out. Addy's shrill little voice follows me to the trunk, where I dig out a bottle, powdered formula, and a jug of distilled water.

I fumble the oversize can of formula as I peel the aluminum off the top. Half the can spills out onto the parking lot.

"Shit. This shit cost me twenty-five bucks."

Addy's screams reach a glass-shattering pitch.

"I'm coming! It's okay!" I read the back of the can for mixing instructions and realize I have no idea how much to give her. I start to panic. *Calm down,* I tell myself. *It's baby formula. It can't be that hard.* I take a few deep breaths, trying to block out the insanely loud screaming from the backseat that makes me want to hide under the car, and decide to make four ounces. I can always make more if I need to.

After screwing on the top of the bottle, I shake it up as I make my way back around to the driver's-side door and push the seat forward.

"Hi, sweet pea." Her face is beet red, and her tongue vibrates as she yells. I unbuckle her and pick her up. She screams in my ear, then turns her head, finds my cheek with her mouth, and starts sucking.

"Okay, Addy baby, that's not going to get you anywhere. Come here." I cradle her in the crook of my arm and put the bottle's nipple into her mouth. She sucks and sucks and sucks. It looks like her head might explode. Then she opens her mouth and howls like her pants are on fire.

"What? Why aren't you drinking it?" I'm two seconds from freaking out and screaming with her. Why do people have babies? This is insane!

I shake the bottle. Nothing. I yank on the nipple, sure a stream of white baby formula will shoot out, but nothing does. "What the heck?"

I turn the bottle over and examine the nipple. "Well, no wonder. This stupid nipple isn't even cut all the way open. Damn it."

By this time, I'm really afraid she's going to burst a couple of blood vessels in her face, she's crying so hard. I've gone from frustrated to scared out of my mind that I'll need to take her back to the hospital because I've broken her—she's never going to stop screaming. I sit her back in her car seat and hustle to the trunk again to get a different nipple.

Finally, I'm in the backseat again with Addy in my arms, and she's ecstatic. Her eyes are closed and she's sucking the formula down so fast, I'm sure she was starving. When it's gone, I take the bottle out of her mouth. Her lips still make their sucking motion, and her eyes stay closed. I put her over my shoulder and pat her back gently.

I don't get a burp. I get a deluge. She pukes up what has to be all four ounces all over me, the backseat, and herself, and starts crying again. Formula is coming out her nose. Suddenly I remember what I forgot to buy. Burp cloths.

Looking around the rest area, I don't see anyone close to us or paying attention. I whip my T-shirt over my head and wipe her face with it. Then I sit her in her car seat and make a mad dash to the trunk again to get us both clean clothes. I also grab a diaper and a pacifier.

What I thought would be a fifteen-minute stop has turned into an hour. As I pull the car away, Addy calm and asleep in fresh clothes and diaper, I admit to myself that I'm in way over my head. One pit stop and I'm almost in tears.

Six o'clock. At this rate, we'll get to Florida in about a week.

We stop again at eight and ten. Both times, Addy pukes all over herself, the car seat, and me. I make a mental note to purchase a rain poncho for feeding time once we get to Florida. We have so much time to make up on the road, I'm not stopping for any reason other than to feed her. Luckily, newborns sleep a lot, so her crying sprees are limited to two-hour intervals.

We're almost through North Carolina when red and blue lights start flashing behind me. I think I've swallowed my tongue, and I hold my breath as I pull off to the right side of the highway. My heart is attempting to punch and kick its way out of my chest.

"Shit, shit, shit." I open the glove box and dig around for Mom's registration. I know there's no proof of insurance, but it won't hurt to pretend I'm searching my ass off for a card. If Mom filed a police report on me, I'm fucked.

Sweat beads on my forehead and the back of my neck. I

jump when the officer knocks on my window and drop the eight hundred folded and wadded-up pieces of paper I'm clutching. Addy starts whimpering in the back.

My hand cranks down the window as I peer into the backseat. She's winding up, getting louder.

"Shh, Addy, don't cry." I reach back and pat her cookie-size foot.

"Miss, please don't reach into the backseat," the officer says with his deep, all-official voice.

Addy ups the pitch and tone.

My pulse races.

I flip around to the officer. "I'm *just* trying to keep her from completely freaking out, okay?"

But it's too late. Addy's out of control. She's started to hiccup, and that makes her mad, which makes her belt out the loudest screams I can even imagine. My ears are bleeding.

Pissed, I turn on the cop. "Do you see what you've done? I hope whatever reason you have for pulling me over is worth it. I know I wasn't going over the speed limit."

"You have a taillight out. Just get it fixed." He tips his hat and marches back to his cruiser.

"Sweet Jesus. Addy, you are the coolest baby ever." I wipe the sweat off my forehead as the cop car pulls back onto the highway and disappears from sight.

For a while, I just sit and breathe, listening to Addy suck in air, scream until her lungs deflate with a little hiss, then gasp for air again. After five minutes, she's worn out and falls asleep, and I pull back onto the highway, knuckles white, heart all beat out.

At eight in the morning we reach Jacksonville, Florida, and I pull into the first budget motel my eyes spot off the highway. I drag myself out of the car, flip up my seat, and unbuckle Addy.

I carry her into the motel office. It's filled with the pungent smells of hot electrical wires and hot dogs with onions. Addy squirms in my arms when I ring the bell that sits on the scratched-up counter.

An older man in need of a shave, with dark gray wiry hair, comes out of the back room. "Help you?"

"I need a room for a couple of nights."

His fingers clack on the computer keyboard. "Okay, just the two of you?"

I glance down at Addy. Her deep blue eyes are watching me. "Yeah, just the two of us."

"That's eighty dollars a night plus tax." He's printing up the receipt as my mouth drops open. Eighty dollars a night? Plus tax.

"Will that be cash or credit card?"

A huge, tired, regretful sigh escapes my lungs. "Cash." I juggle Addy and my bag, trying to unzip one while not dropping the other.

The old man watches me, obviously entertained.

"Don't worry. I got it." I toss the money on the counter. He makes change and slides it along with the key across the counter.

"Have a good morning." He's already on his way to the back again.

I push the door open with my butt, wrestle with the straps on Addy's car seat, and drive us around the building to room 210. I'm exhausted and thankful Addy can't roll over, so I can leave her lying in the middle of the bed while I make a couple of trips to the car to unload only our necessities from the trunk.

For someone so small, she sure needs a lot of crap.

I kick off my shoes and lie down beside her. Her arms and legs flail around with jerky movements, like she has absolutely no control over them. Every once in a while she makes a clucking noise with her tongue.

I grab the remote off the nightstand and turn the TV on. *Sesame Street* is the first show that fills the screen. "Perfect."

The next thing I know, Addy's crying and it's four hours later. "Oh, Addster, you let me sleep four hours. You're such a good baby." I give her my finger, and she holds on to it with her baby kung fu grip.

I feed her, she pukes, and I run a warm bath for her. She lies in the bottom of the tub in a half inch of water, kicking and making happy baby noises. I could eat her cheeks they're so chubby and cute.

Her toes remind me of corn kernels, and she has chubby sausages for thighs. She's a baby buffet. Even if she's half my mom's, she's the most beautiful baby I've ever seen. She really does look like Hope, except for the dark hair.

A wave of homesickness washes over me. Well, not homesickness exactly. I don't care if I ever go back there, but I miss Hope like crazy. I almost told her my plan. But she'd never have let me do it.

She wouldn't have understood.

She already found her way out.

I needed a shove out of that hellhole. Addy gave me motivation to escape, in one soft, squishy package.

The soap between my hands foams and bubbles as I rub them together. Addy's eyes widen, following my fast motions. She's more alert than I'd thought a newborn would be. Of course, she sleeps most of the day, but when she's awake, she's looking around with this expression on her face like, *Where the heck am I?*

I soap and rinse her, careful not to get her umbilical cord wet, then lift her out of the tub. She startles, arms shooting out and her face looking panic stricken.

"I won't drop you, sweet pea, don't worry." I rest her against me, where I've thrown a towel across my chest, and wrap the ends around her.

"After we get you dressed, we'll try out your stroller." I lay her back in the middle of the bed while I dig in the diaper bag for a clean outfit. She only has a handful and has puked on most of them. "We need to find a Laundromat or a thrift store."

As I put Addy's diaper on, I wonder how pissed Mom is. The cops have to be looking for me—no, the cops have to be looking for Addy. Mom doesn't care if I disappear, but Addy's her meal ticket. Her weed ticket.

I run my fingers over the soft fuzz on top of Addy's head. "You're worth more than that." I wonder if Dave and Angel have filed a police report too.

Probably.

I'm screwed.

I snap Addy's romper, and my stomach twists. A rush of nervous energy shoots through me. I shake out my hands and take deep breaths. I need to get out of here for a little while.

"Okay, let's go for a walk, Addster."

I leave her in the center of the bed, kicking and trying to find her mouth with her fist, while I pick up the folded stroller propped in the corner. In the open space by the door, I attempt to unfold it. It doesn't budge. I tug harder. Nothing.

I stomp my foot onto the bar attaching the wheels together to steady the stroller before yanking and pulling with all my might. It still doesn't budge, but a piece of the plastic handle breaks off in my hand. I toss the broken bit onto the table and kick the stroller.

"Damn it." I wipe my forehead across my shoulder and plop onto the bed. Addy's tummy is warm under my hand. "Add, I don't even know how to open your stroller." I shake my head. "I suck at this. We have to find someone who can take care of you."

But the thought of parting with her is like tearing off one of my limbs. I pick her up and press my face into her neck. I love her baby smell, the soft new skin, the milky breath. The weight of her, a little bag of flour in my arms, is comfort and home to me—just like that. It's been one day, and I can't live without her. She's *my* baby.

I peer at my nemesis, the stroller, resting staunch and resolute against the door. A silver latch gleams at me, mocking.

"You've got to be kidding."

I slump over to the stroller, entirely defeated, and slide the latch. The stroller falls open and clicks into place. When I wrap my hands around the handles, the sharp, broken edge presses against my left palm.

The next fifteen minutes are spent finding something to cover the broken handle with so I can push the stroller. Finally, after I figure out that a sock makes the most sense, I take another five minutes to pack a diaper bag and stash it in the net basket under the stroller.

I groan as my eyes run over Addy. Legs kicking in the air, her yellow romper is darker in color around the rear. My suspicion's confirmed when I feel the soft cotton—it's wet. Another fifteen minutes go by while I change her, wipe her, and dress her for the second time today.

It seems like half the day has passed when at last I'm buckling her into the stroller—and she starts crying. First it's a small whine, but soon it's a full-out scream fest. I look at the clock. It's been two hours since her last bottle.

My head drops into my hands with the realization that my world now revolves in two-hour increments. Two hours used to seem like such a long time, but that was before the clock was always on my back counting down.

Addy's earsplitting shrieks pierce through my skull as I carry her toward the dresser on the back wall, where I organized her bottles, powdered formula, and distilled water. I bounce her in one arm while making a bottle with the other. I'm getting better at one-handed bottle making. After it's been in the microwave for ten seconds, I shake the bottle fiercely to make sure there are no hot spots, then stuff the nipple in her mouth.

She sucks and snuffles air through her nose, trying to eat and catch her breath at the same time. Her arm is out to the side, up in the air. Her hand opens and closes, opens and closes.

I settle into a chair at the small table by the door and watch her finish the bottle. When she's done, I take it from her mouth and put it on the table. Just like always, her lips still form their little O and make their sucking motion. Her eyes are closed, and she sighs.

A knock on the door startles her, and her eyes pop open. For a second I think she'll go back to sleep, but then her mouth opens wide and she starts wailing as I dart toward the door and look out.

The old man who checked us in is visible through the peephole. I open the door and smile. "Hello," I shout over Addy's cries.

He's frowning. "We have a problem," he says.

chapter

six

Every muscle in my body stiffens, and my skin tingles with anxiety. I hold Addy closer, tighter.

"What's the problem?" My voice is too high. I'm going to give us away if I don't play it cool.

My eyes dart to the parking lot behind him, fully expecting to see a whole parade of cop cars pulling in any second, sirens blaring, light bars flashing blue and red.

"I'm getting complaints about your baby crying."

"My baby?" I look down at Addy. "She doesn't cry that much, only when she's hungry. I make her bottles as fast as I can."

Addy starts squirming and hiccupping between her blasts of cries. I forgot to burp her. If I burp her, she'll puke everywhere. My nerve endings climb up and seethe just under my skin, threatening to burst through. My breathing turns to ragged gasps that I hold back, willing myself to stay calm until he's gone.

"I'm getting complaints, and it's not even night yet. I don't want to think about what's going to happen when she wakes up at three in the morning screaming." His eyes roll skyward, like he's praying, or contemplating going home sick and not dealing with the irate customers bitching about the ballistic baby screaming in 210.

"Um. Okay." I don't know what to tell him. Where am I supposed to go?

" 'Okay,' what?" His eyes snap back to my face.

"I don't know. Are you kicking us out? Should we find a parking lot and sleep in the car?" I gesture to Addy, hoping no sane person would ask me to sleep in a car with a newborn.

He clenches his hands into fists. "No. Of course not." He looks down and shakes his head. "If the motel wasn't full, I could put you on an end, by yourselves. How long are you planning on staying?"

I shrug. "Until I find us a more permanent place. We just moved here."

He picks up a newspaper at his feet on the sidewalk and shoves it into my free hand. "Well, take a look in the paper. There's bound to be some place for rent in there. In the meantime, try to keep the kid quiet."

Without waiting for a response, he shuffles down the sidewalk, and I shut the door.

As predicted, two pats on Addy's back, and I'm covered in puke. I lay her back on the bed, change my shirt, and wad it up with more of our disgusting, crusty, puked-on clothes. After stuffing them into her diaper bag, I buckle her in the stroller and we head out, in search of a Laundromat.

The sun's hot, and it hazes off the blacktop. I squint and toss a lightweight blanket over the stroller to shield Addy's eyes. I push her slowly, enjoying the heat, letting it pulse through my body, into my muscles.

At the end of the parking lot, semis rush past on the busy road, throwing up cinders and dirt. There's no sidewalk. I visualize pushing the stroller down the side of the road, over the sand and cinders and broken bottles and God only knows what else. Another semi flies past, making it clear that I'm not taking the stroller anywhere beyond this parking lot.

Addy and I head back across the lot to the car. I open the door to fasten her in her seat before I stash the stroller in the trunk, but a gust of air too hot to breathe rushes out at us from inside the car. Having a baby is insanely complicated. Even the most mundane tasks, like getting in the car, take ten steps to accomplish.

After hauling her back inside the room and situating her in the center of the bed, I run out and start the car, blasting the air conditioner. I toss the newspaper onto the passenger seat and can't pull my eyes from it.

Our future is in there somewhere. It has to be. Those pages hold the key to us making it together, Addy and me, against the world. My fingers run over the smooth, black-and-white front page.

The paper back home probably has an article about the delinquent teen who stole a baby from the hospital. I grip the steering wheel. I have to ditch this car somehow. The Ohio plates are a flashing beacon: *Here she is! Come arrest her and take the baby.*

Cool air begins to blow from the vents, so I hop out of the car to get Addy. Once we're finally buckled in and pulling out of the motel lot, I feel much better. We're back on track.

A half mile down the road, there's a sign with a green-skinned cartoon witch on it. Green Witch Soap and Suds. It's a small building with curtained windows around the front and sides. Gravel crunches under my tires as I find a spot and park. I gather the newspaper, diaper bag, and Addy and cross the parking lot to the door. Through the glass, I see tables, and a bar with stools. Beyond that, there's another glass door. Coin-operated washing machines stand on the opposite side. Soap and Suds. I get it. Suds is for the beer. Soap is for the laundry.

I shove the door open, and the bell attached to the top tinkles. There's a middle-aged man at the bar drinking a bottle of beer and talking with a waitress old enough to be his mother. They're the only two in the place.

"Hello, dear!" the waitress calls, and digs in her pocket, a moment later producing an order pad. "What can I get you?" When she realizes the little ball in my arms isn't just dirty laundry, she practically jumps the counter to get over to the table where I'm sitting with the diaper bag and newspaper. She's pretty fast for an old lady.

"Oh my! How old is she? She's just precious. I haven't been around one this tiny in a long time."

"She's . . ." I pause, wondering if I should say she's barely two days old. I decide against it—better to keep up with the lie. "She's two months old."

"Really?" The woman peers down at Addy, who's asleep in my arms. "She's so small."

"She was premature." I turn my body and sit so the woman can't scrutinize Addy anymore. "Can I have some coffee, please?" My stomach grumbles at the smell of the greasy food I'm inhaling. It's just past two o'clock, and I haven't eaten in . . . I can't remember how long. "And a cheeseburger with fries."

The woman marks her order pad. "Shouldn't take too long. If you have clothes to put in"—she gestures through the glass door to the adjoining room—"go ahead. You can leave your diaper bag here. I'll keep an eye on it."

She walks away while I shift Addy to my other arm, grab the diaper bag, which has our laundry in it, and head toward the connecting door.

I juggle Addy, trying to unzip the bag without dropping her. I finally get it open and toss the laundry into a machine. Then I realize I need some change, not only for the machine but also for the detergent dispenser on the wall.

Back through the door, I ask the waitress for quarters. She digs in her apron and produces a couple dollars' worth, and I hand her two ones.

"Can I hold her while you start up the washer? I'll come back there with you."

"Yes, that would be great." Relieved with her offer, I head back to my dirty clothes with her on my heels. "I can't believe how much harder everything is with a baby." Standing at the machine, I hand Addy over to the woman.

"You don't have to tell me." She makes cooing baby noises at Addy. "I had five of my own. I moved here three years ago to help care for my mother. Now I never see them, or my grandkids."

I feel like a wart on the ass of humanity standing here with this woman who gave up so much to help her mom when I just screwed mine over so royally. She catches the expression on my face. "What's wrong? Are you okay?"

I nod and turn toward the detergent dispenser on the wall beside the door. I will *not* feel bad about giving my mother what she deserves, about giving her back some of the shit she's dealt me my whole life.

I dump in three quarters and jab the button for Tide. The waitress is over by the washing machine, shaking her head.

"You can't put whites in with jeans. Everything's going to turn blue. Here." She settles Addy into my arms, grabs the detergent out of my hands, digs the whites out, and tosses them into the next washer.

"But, I don't—" I don't have the money to do two loads.

She waves me off, digs in her apron, and pulls out more quarters. "I'm Ivy, by the way."

"Thanks. I'm . . ." I can't tell her my name is Faith. What if she finds out I'm a babynapper and turns me in? "Leah. I'm Leah." It's my middle name.

She smiles and runs a finger down Addy's cheek. "What about this little one? What's her name?"

"Addy."

"Very pretty. And old-fashioned. My grandmother had a cousin named Addy." She shakes the powdered soap into both washers and starts them. "Come on. Let's see if your burger's ready."

Sitting sideways back at the table, I prop my legs up on the chair next to me and lay a sleeping Addy in the divot between my knees.

Ivy comes over and sets a plate piled high with fries on the table in front of me. The cheeseburger is barely visible under the crispy heap. Then she places a dish of coleslaw down beside it.

"You need vegetables to keep up your strength. It's not easy raising a little one."

I shrug. "Got fries. Potatoes are vegetables."

She smacks my shoulder with the dishtowel she used to

carry the hot plate to my table. "Don't be a smarty-pants." Then she slides into the chair across from me.

I make an empty spot on the side of my plate, twist the lid off the ketchup, and turn the bottle over. Ivy's staring at Addy, who purses her mouth in a sucking motion, dreaming of her bottle.

Ignoring them both, I snatch up the newspaper and flip to the Furnished Rooms for Rent section of the classifieds.

Addy and I are like birds that flee to Florida in the winter, looking for a warm, safe spot to land. There has to be a place for us somewhere.

"Looking for a place to live?"

I tip the newspaper and peer over the top. "Yeah." I eye her warily. What if she knows about us? It might be on the news. There could be an Amber Alert out for Addy.

"Well, this is perfect!" She slaps her palm on the speckled Formica tabletop. "My nephew's got his upstairs for rent. I'll give him a call. He lives over in Jasper. It's a cute little town. You'll love it."

I'm just about to argue, not wanting this woman to be able to pinpoint our exact whereabouts, when she adds, "It's the perfect town for raising children—great schools and parks, nice neighborhoods."

I peer down at Addy as Ivy pushes herself to her feet. "Think you can make it out there today to take a look if my nephew will be around?"

Addy's face scrunches up and she yawns, letting out the smallest sigh. "Yeah," I say. "I can make it out there today."

I slow the car, searching house numbers for 356 Maple Street. The neighborhood is like something out of a movie: tree-lined streets, sidewalks, and picket fences. Nothing bad could ever happen here. It's a place where wishes and prayers could actually come true. This is what Addy deserves.

My eyes spot the address I'm searching for on a green plastic mailbox. "Here it is," I whisper to Addy. "Cross your fingers." The rear tires bump over the curb as I turn the car into the short driveway, which leads to a two-car garage. The house is a tidy, white cape cod with a black door and shutters. Dark green awnings shade the windows, making the house look like it has droopy, tired eyes.

My hand grips the gearshift, and I put the car in park. I'm clenching my stomach so tightly, I feel like I might pass out. I close my eyes and take a deep breath, holding it for ten seconds, and then blow it out hard and fast. I do this a few more times and the dizziness subsides. "Okay, Add, let's go."

The warm bundle of baby in my arms, pressed against my chest, is reality, security. She grounds me. She gives my feet purpose to stumble up the sidewalk and onto the front stoop without turning around and running back to the car.

I open the screen door and knock.

My heart beats so loudly, I can hear it pounding in my ears.

I wait.

There's music inside, a faint strumming.

I press the doorbell and listen to it chime.

The strumming stops.

Footsteps approach the door.

I squeeze Addy closer. She whines.

The door is tugged open.

"Hey. Leah, right?" The boy standing in the doorway can't be more than a few years older than me. He holds a guitar in the hand that's not gripping the doorknob.

I nod. I can't speak.

He stands back and gestures me inside. "My dad's not here, but Aunt Ivy talked to him. He called to let me know you'd be stopping by."

I follow him through the family room with its golden-tan carpet and beige couch and love seat. A can of Coke sits on a coaster on the coffee table.

"Room's upstairs," he says, and I notice the staircase between the family room and the kitchen, which has sunny yellow walls.

I climb the stairs behind him. His jeans are worn and hang low on his hips. His T-shirt's gray—the cotton would be soft to touch.

At the top, he opens a door and steps inside. It's one massive room. "Go ahead and look around," he says, and plops down on a blue couch against the wall between two deep-set dormer windows. He tugs a rubber band and a guitar pick from his front pocket and holds the pick between his front teeth as he pulls his chin-length dirty-blond hair back into a stubby ponytail.

There isn't anywhere to go. But I turn toward a row of oak cabinets with a laminate countertop lining the back wall. There's a tiny, bar-size sink and a minifridge. A small table with two chairs sits in front of them.

"Couch pulls out to a bed," he says.

I run my hand over the counter and feel gritty dust on my fingers.

The boy strums his guitar.

Sun shines through the window over the sink.

Addy wriggles and pops her arm out from under her, holding it up in the air.

"What's your baby's name?" the boy asks over his guitar.

"Addy."

"I'm Chris." His eyes are blue-green. They'd be bluer or greener depending on what he wore. His gray shirt keeps them the in-between shade. He plays a few more chords and sets his guitar beside him on the couch. "Well? What do you think?"

I glance around. There's not much to it, but it works. "How much?"

He rubs his chin. It's covered in stubble. I imagine how it would feel against my cheek, and my face gets hot.

Addy squirms and lets out a small shriek. Chris's eyes dart to her. This could be the deal breaker.

She squawks again. "What time is it?" I ask, realizing she's probably hungry.

He shrugs. "Around five or six. She need to eat?"

"Yeah. Guess I better go so I can feed her." I take a step toward the door.

"Here." He comes forward, reaching his arms out. "I'll hold her. Go on out and get her a bottle. You have one with you, don't you?"

I nod, watching him take Addy out of my arms, place her against his chest, and rub her back. "Do you have kids?" It seems like a dumb question, but he's a natural with Addy.

He laughs. "No. Fortunately, I've never been in that predicament." He looks from Addy to me, and his face falls. "I mean . . ."

Right. He thinks I got knocked up. I'm a teen mom. "It's okay. Don't worry about it." I smile, trying to put him at ease. "I'll be right back."

After opening the door to the stairs, I glance over my shoulder. He's running his fingers over the top of her head and bouncing her gently. "Shh, baby, don't cry. Mommy will be right back."

Running down the stairs, I ponder the likelihood of something inside me actually melting, because I'm certain something has. Something I didn't even know was frozen.

I dash outside, grab the diaper bag off of the passenger seat, and run back into the house. Upstairs, Chris is standing in front of one of the dormer windows, talking to Addy as he rocks back and forth. "That's an oak tree. Squirrels love that tree. They hide acorns in it."

He hears me at the door, and he turns. "There she is," he tells Addy.

I blink about a thousand times, trying to take in the image in front of me, overwhelmed with so many emotions. The sun streams in behind him, catching strands of his hair, reminding me of how Hope looked sitting in Brian's car on our way to school. Addy's comfortable and content in his arms—like she belongs there.

We belong here.

"What's wrong?" he asks.

I shake my head. "Nothing. Thanks for holding her. I just need to mix it up." I point to the counter.

"Sure. Take your time. We're fine." He turns back to the window, and I can't stop staring.

For the first time since I took Addy away, it feels like I did the right thing. And I'm not just telling myself that. It's true. I can give her this life. The life she deserves.

Some of the powdered formula falls over the sides of the bottle as I pour it in. I swipe it into the sink with my hand. Addy starts to fuss again as I'm pouring the water into her bottle. I screw on the nipple and shake the bottle up as I walk toward her and Chris.

"Need to warm it up?" His eyes meet mine. I see myself in them. Not just my reflection. He's giving me everything I desperately need. And I'm giving him something too. But I have no idea what. I just know that I can see it in his eyes, the yearning to keep me there with him, to keep *us* with him.

"Um . . ." I hadn't thought to warm it this time. I'm a terrible mom.

"Trade ya." He smiles and takes the bottle, handing Addy over into my arms. "I'll hurry."

I lower onto the couch, hugging Addy to me, nuzzling my nose against her neck. There's a smell there I'm not familiar with. It's male. It's dizzying. It's Chris.

A microwave beeps downstairs, and a second later his feet are padding up the steps. He rushes through the door, and I feel my lips automatically turn up into a smile.

His hair's down now, framing his face. The rubber band grips his wrist. He hands me the bottle and sits beside me. "I tested it."

Addy starts sucking. Chris gives her his finger to clutch. She moves her eyes around, searching, for him I think. Then she scarfs the formula down.

We don't speak.

We just watch her eat.

When she's done, Chris takes the bottle from me and goes over to the sink to rinse it out.

Before I even have her over my shoulder to burp her, she pukes all over my shirt. Chris turns around and cracks up at seeing me all wet and gross. "Well, that just sucks." He laughs some more. "Hang on. I'll get you a T-shirt to borrow."

He jogs down the stairs and comes back a minute later with a faded black T-shirt that reads LORD OF THE STRINGS and has a picture of a guitar on it. I take it from him and stand up. Since there's nowhere to go to change, I just stand there and wait for him to leave.

"Oh," he finally says, getting it. "I'll take her downstairs and wait for you." Just as he's about to take Addy from me, he stops and smiles. "Just a sec." He goes to the cupboard, pulls out a roll of paper towels, runs one under the faucet, and comes back to me. "Got a little in your hair." He takes the strands of my hair between two fingers and gently wipes away the baby vomit. "Better."

Chris and Addy head downstairs, with him chattering to her the whole way. I tug off my gross shirt and pull on his. It's as soft as I imagine the one he's wearing to be and has the smell that he left on Addy. A faint manly scent, like aftershave.

I take a deep breath and hold it in, letting it fill my head. What is it about him that tells me I'm on the right path?

I swing the diaper bag over my shoulder and am about to leave when I see his guitar sitting on the couch. I run my fingers over it. It's smooth and slick. I carefully pick it up and take it down the stairs with me.

He's taking a swig of Coke when I get to the bottom of the steps. Addy's lying beside him on the couch. His hand's on her stomach, fingers curling and uncurling, massaging her tummy. She hiccups and lets out an irritated squeal.

"I know. You hate hiccups. It's okay, they'll go away soon."

He puts the Coke down when he sees me and pushes his hair back behind his ear. "So, when are you moving in?"

I can't help but smile. I know being here with him would transform my life for the better. "I don't know if I can afford it. How much is it a month?" I place the guitar against the coffee table, beside his feet.

"Well, for a friend of Aunt Ivy, a hundred bucks."

My eyes almost fall out of my head. "A month? That's it?"

He shrugs. "Sure. We're not using it."

"Should you . . ." I pause, sticking my hands in my back

pockets and watching my shoes as I push up and down on my toes. "Shouldn't you make sure it's okay with your dad?"

He shakes his head. "He won't care. He's never here. It was my idea to rent out the upstairs, anyway. It goes toward my college fund—if I ever go back."

"Wow. Okay, yeah. How soon can I move in?" An anxious buzz flits through my chest.

He smiles and looks around. "How about now? I don't see anyone else claiming it." Then he laughs. "If you need help, I have a pickup."

I shake my head. "We don't have very much stuff."

He tilts his head, curiosity clear in his eyes. "Where are you from?"

Uh-oh. Here come the questions. "Ohio."

"How long have you been in Florida?"

I pick Addy up off the couch and walk her around the room, needing to do something other than stand under his scrutinizing eyes. "Not very long."

"Okay. I get it. You don't want to talk about it. I respect that."

I turn my head toward him. He's got his guitar on his lap. "It's just . . ."

He smiles, but only one side of his mouth raises. "It's cool. You don't have to tell me. I can watch her if you want to go get the rest of your stuff."

My thoughts shift to the upstairs, filling in all the empty places with things I'll need to buy to make it livable—towels, sheets, pillows, a clock. Addy's asleep and breathing deeply, letting out little *pft, pft, pft* sounds. "It's already getting late. How about I move in tomorrow?"

"I work till five, but my dad should be here before that. I'll let him know you're coming, though."

I take a deep breath and exhale, nervous about The Dad. Since I've never had one around myself, I'm not too sure what to expect.

Chris looks up from his guitar. "Don't worry, he's cool. He doesn't talk a lot or hang around, just keeps to himself pretty much." He beats the front of his guitar with his palm, making a hollow echo.

"All right, then, guess I'll see you tomorrow."

Chris walks us to the door, then surprises me by following us to my car. He stands in the driveway while I situate Addy in her car seat.

Before I get in, I stand there, feeling awkward. A hug would be inappropriate, even though it feels like it'd be the right thing to do. A handshake seems way too formal. After a moment, I decide to just get in the car.

Chris puts his hand on the door handle and waits until I'm buckled in. "I'm glad you're going to be living upstairs. See ya tomorrow." Then he closes my car door and takes a step back onto the walkway, where he watches me back out and drive down the street. Through the rearview mirror, I watch him watching me until I turn the corner and he's out of sight.

chapter

seven

The day offers up something else for me to be thankful for—a large changing station in the ladies' room at Walmart. Driving from our new house to the motel, Addy stinks up the car so bad, I almost wreck.

After changing her, I toss the dirty diaper into the trash and button her back up. "Pillows, towels, sheets. Can you remember that, Add?"

"Pillows, towels, sheets," I tell myself over and over.

Outside the bathroom, I grab a cart one-handed and realize that it's going to be next to impossible to carry Addy, shop, and push a cart. But I have no choice. I also have no clue how other mothers do this all the time, but I'm about to find out.

It's slow going, but I maneuver the cart to the aisle with towels and pull two ivory-colored ones off the shelf.

The whole pile falls onto the floor.

I bend to pick them up and whack my head on the cart.

Addy starts whining, upset that I'm holding her sideways.

I leave the towels that fell, grab two washcloths, and head toward the sheets.

Tired and fussy, Addy screams her brains out the entire way through the store. I stop in the baby aisle to stock up, but my mind is panicked and scattered, and I don't even know if I got everything I need. The checkout lines are three and four people deep, and I have to stand there forever with everybody scowling at me and banshee baby, who keeps spitting out her pacifier.

When it's finally our turn and the cashier rings everything up, I want to scream as loud as Addy at the total on the screen. "One hundred thirty-four dollars and sixty-three cents," the lady tells me as she folds the last washcloth and stuffs it into a plastic bag.

I peel back twenty-dollar bills from the wad of cash in my wallet, feeling like I'm handing over fingers and toes.

I'd rather be handing over fingers and toes—where am I going to get more money?

"Are you hiring?" I ask her.

"I'm sorry? . . ." She cups her ear and darts a glance at Addy, who's all quivering lips and tonsils.

I shake my head, mouth *never mind*, and hand her the money. I'll stop back when crazy baby is calm.

Addy falls asleep on the car ride back to the motel. I realize I'm exhausted, and it's only nine o'clock.

I give Addy a bottle and let her make a mess on the towel I draped over myself before I undress her and wash her off with a warm cloth. I'm starting to worry that there's something wrong with her. Tomorrow, I'll ask Chris if he has a computer, then I'll Google "babies puking after every bottle" to see if she's defective.

God, I hope not. That would mean taking her to the doctor and answering a barrage of questions about me being her mom. They might want a birth certificate. Plus, I don't have enough money if she needs surgery or something. I suck at this.

My fingernail starts bleeding when I bite it down to the quick. I suck on it until the blood stops.

I can't do this.

I can't worry about things that might never happen.

I have enough to keep my stomach in knots as it is.

With Addy's pajamas on her, I lay her on the bed to put mine on. But after stripping off my jeans, I can't bring myself to remove Chris's T-shirt. So, I keep it on and crawl into bed.

I hate that some boy I don't even know can make me feel like Addy and I have been saved. Like he'd take a bullet for us or something. I pinch the squishy skin between my thumb and forefinger. "Don't be a fucking idiot," I whisper to myself, then bite my lips and remind myself to never cuss around Addy.

Even if she can't repeat after me yet, it's best to get out of the habit now.

Between the semis rushing by, ambulance and police sirens blaring, and the occasional late check-in dragging a suitcase down the sidewalk, I listen to the soft intake of Addy's breath, then the ruffle of her exhale. There's no other sound like it on earth.

I slide closer, rest my fingers over her tiny arm, and press my nose against her chubby cheek. Before falling asleep, I think about how everything is going to be perfect.

At two in the morning, Addy wakes up shrieking. I feed and change her, but no matter what I do, she won't stop crying. I pace the room, bouncing her and holding the pacifier in her mouth. She can't seem to keep it between her lips without it popping out, which makes her even angrier.

Our neighbors on all sides pound on the walls and shout at me to *shut that baby up!*

I know it's only a matter of minutes before the old man from the front office comes to our room, demanding that we leave. I shove my feet into my flip-flops, grab the diaper bag and my keys, pick up Addy, and dart out the door. We'll drive around until morning, or until she stops crying, whichever comes first.

As I buckle her in, I see him coming down the sidewalk. Before he can get a word out, I call to him, "I'm sorry. I'm taking her for a drive. We'll check out in the morning. I found a place for us to live."

He frowns, waves me off, and turns back toward the front office.

Without having anywhere else to go, I drive to Jasper, past our new house. Addy isn't screaming anymore, but her sleep is restless. Every once in a while, she lets out a shriek.

I slow the car as we approach 356 Maple Street. The lights upstairs, in our room, are on. A shadow passes the window, and I strain to see inside. Chris comes into view. His hair's pulled back. He's shirtless, and there's a paintbrush in his hand.

I stop at the curb and watch, hoping he won't look out and see the car. He's singing, and every once in a while he uses the paintbrush as a microphone.

I laugh, and it echoes through the car. Addy shifts in her car seat but stays asleep.

Chris bends, disappearing from sight for a second, then straightens and raises a Coke can to his lips as he wipes his chest with a white paint rag. A tool belt hugs his hips.

I feel hot all of a sudden and crack my window. My forehead's slick, and I wipe it with the bottom of his T-shirt.

I don't want to leave, but the longer I stay, the higher my chances of being caught spying on him.

It's five thirty in the morning when I pull back into the motel parking lot. I give Addy a bottle in the car before we go back into our room. I catch her puke in a diaper and pitch it into the trash can out on the sidewalk.

Checkout isn't until eleven, so I crawl back into bed with Addy. Her 2:00 a.m. crying fit must've worn her out, because she sleeps soundly, and it's almost ten when we wake up again.

I shower, pack us up, and leave the key at the front desk with the day clerk. "We're on our way to our own place, Addster!" I tell her as we pull out of the motel parking lot. Hearing the excitement in my voice makes me panic a little bit. I should be wary, nervous, anxious, even guilty, but not excited. There's still the threat of getting caught, not to mention that I don't have a way to support the two of us. Being excited is stupid—I haven't escaped anything yet.

As if to prove my point, when we get to the house, there's a note on the door with my name on it.

Leah,

I'm sorry. I would've called, but I didn't know how to reach you.

My dad doesn't want to rent to someone with a baby. You were right. I should've asked him first. I feel like a jerk.

I'm really sorry.

Chris

I'm clutching the paper so tight, it shakes in my hand.

What am I going to do?

What the hell am I going to do?

I'm breathing hard, and spots of light are flashing in my eyes. I'm about to pass out.

I ease down onto the porch step with Addy asleep against my shoulder.

"I give up," I whisper. "I give up. I can't do this anymore."

My eyes blur with tears, and I close them. I don't want to feel them trailing down my cheeks, but I do.

I can't go back to the motel. I can't stay here. Where else can we go?

I think about home, the feel of the dirty, gummy carpet under my feet, the water that smells like rotten eggs and turns the toilet bowl orange, the smell of smoke that clings to my clothes and hair.

Mom high.

Mom drunk.

I shake my head. I'm not going back there. I'm not taking Addy back there. This is my way out, and it has to work. It's my only chance.

"Come on, Addy," I say, standing up. "Let's get out of here."

I let Chris's note drift to the ground and watch it blow across the grass.

With nothing else to do, I drive around for a while thinking, trying to come up with a new plan. We're going to have to stay at a hotel until I can find us another place to live.

I stop at a Quality Inn and lug Addy inside. Going from the bright, hot sun in the car and parking lot, to the dim, air-conditioned lobby makes her startle awake. She blinks and yawns. I hold my breath, praying she doesn't start crying.

Luckily, she closes her eyes again and falls back asleep.

"Can I help you?" There's a woman in a blue blazer and a crisp white shirt behind the front desk.

I step up to the desk and clear my throat. "Yes. I'd like to know how much a room would be for the night."

"I'm sorry, we don't have any available rooms for the next two days. There's a big televangelist convention in Jacksonville with a bunch of those TV ministers." She waits for me to nod, like I know who she's talking about. "Most of the hotels in the area are booked."

"Oh. Okay. Thanks anyway."

I walk back to the car with an instant headache.

I stop at two more hotels and one seedy-looking motel with a dry, cracked in-ground pool taken over by weeds. Even the skanky motel is booked. The fat, sweaty guy behind the desk there tells me that even all the campsites in the area are full. "Good luck," he says, chuckling and shaking his head.

I don't know what to do, so I get back on the highway. Addy starts to fuss, and a look at the clock tells me it's time for a bottle. Since there's nowhere to get off or pull over, I drive with her screaming for another fifteen minutes until I get to a rest stop. It's lucky that they have a drinking fountain, because I didn't make any bottles before we checked out of the hotel this morning, figuring we'd be settled in our new place by now. Stupid me.

Sitting on a bench in the shade, I watch Addy drink her formula. All I wanted to do was give her a nice place to live.

My shoulders and chin feel like gravity is sucking them downward.

I'm sad. Sad and defeated.

But I didn't steal Addy and make it this far to let some baby hater like Mr. Buckridge get the best of me. Maybe if

Chris's dad met Addy, he'd see that she's a good baby and let us live there. After all, Aunt Ivy likes Addy. . . .

It hits me like a box of rocks dropped from the sky. Ivy's my way in. I can hear her with the phone in her hand saying, "He does what I tell him to. I'm his favorite auntie Ivy."

Hope bubbles in my stomach and makes me giddy. I probably shouldn't do it. I shouldn't play Ivy like this, but there's no other way.

Addy and I find the mall and window-shop for the rest of the day. I splurge and buy caramel corn and a soda. At nine thirty Addy needs to be changed and starts crying, but it's not time to head to the car and Green Witch Soap and Suds yet—they don't close until eleven. I still have time to kill since I don't want to get there until Ivy is gone.

In the lower level of the mall, there's a movie theater. We ride down the escalator, with Addy getting louder and louder all the way. Trying to look like I have an urgent situation, I run to the ticket window and point inside the theater. "I need to change her fast! It's dripping out!"

The man at the window looks grossed out and waves me in. "Go ahead. It's to your right!"

I dart into the women's bathroom with Addy and lean my back against the door. "We did it," I tell her. "Let's hope the big plan works as smoothly."

After changing her, I sneak into a movie about bridesmaids who go on a trip for a bachelorette party. It's a good thing Addy sleeps through it, because she's way too young for an R-rated movie. I crack up at the funny parts and try to forget I'm a homeless runaway kidnapper.

When the movie ends, I drive to Green Witch Soap and Suds. It's well past closing time, and the parking lot's empty when I pull in. I pick a spot that's not right up front but not all the way in the back either. I want Ivy to see us when she gets here in the morning.

Addy's asleep, so I don't bother changing her into pajamas; I just leave her in her car seat and tuck a blanket around her. "'Night-night, baby." I kiss her forehead, and she sighs.

It's a long, hot, uncomfortable night. When I leave the windows down, bugs fly in, but I have to leave them cracked at least, or we'll suffocate. There must be ten mosquitoes in the car that I'm trying to squish against the dashboard. Addy's got a big welt on her cheek where she's been bitten. I've given her another bottle already, gotten absolutely no sleep, and it's three in the morning.

By six, I'm contemplating driving back home. But I can't. I don't want to see my mom ever again. "Just a few more hours," I tell myself. I give Addy another bottle and crash out with her on my lap.

A knock on my side window wakes me. "What in God's name are you two doing? Did you sleep here all night?" Ivy grabs the door handle and tries to jerk it open.

I unlock the door and let her open it. "Yeah, we did. All the hotels are booked. I wanted to catch you to say thanks for trying. I appreciate it. It didn't work out, though. Your nephew doesn't want to rent to someone with a baby."

She scowls. "That's the most ridiculous . . . That man . . . I just . . . Come with me!" She lifts Addy off my lap and marches to the door of Green Witch Soap and Suds with her keys jingling.

I follow her inside and sit at the same table I sat at before while she takes Addy around the bar and grabs the phone. While it rings, she plops a kiss on top of Addy's head.

"Christopher," she says, "put your father on, please." She

nods her head a few times. "Oh, yeah, he is in *big* trouble with me."

After a few minutes, she clears her throat. "Good morning, it's your favorite auntie Ivy calling to ask you what on earth you were thinking casting a young mother out onto the street? Do you know they slept in the car last night?"

Her head starts shaking back and forth. "No. I don't care. You're being a stubborn, ridiculous man, and you will rent this room to Leah and Addy, or I'll call in the big guns." She smirks. "Oh, I would. Now, I'm sending Leah back over." She winks at me. "Uh-huh. Then leave a key in the planter." Ivy jiggles Addy on her hip. "Fine, then. Love you too. Buh-bye."

She hangs up and looks at me. "He's leaving your front-door key in the planter on the back patio table."

I rub my eyes and yawn, trying to look humble and not like this whole scheme worked out just like I'd planned. "Are you sure he's okay with it?"

"He's fine with it." She hands Addy over to me and ties her apron around her waist. "Let's get you some breakfast."

"Thanks, Ivy. I don't know what we would've done."

I reach over and hug her with Addy trapped between us, squirming. Even though the appreciation is real, I feel like I have a little bit too much of my mother in me if I can manipulate someone so easily. It makes me feel like there's something vile crawling up my back.

chapter

eight

After finding the key, I open the front door. It feels wrong at first, being in someone else's home without that person there. The home of someone who doesn't want us to be here.

I sit on the couch and dig a baby blanket out of the diaper bag, then spread it out on the tan living room carpet. Addy lies in the middle with her big eyes searching around her. I wonder if she remembers where she is.

She's a good baby and doesn't make a sound as I haul in all her stuff, the Walmart bags from our shopping trip, and my one meager bag of clothes, and sit them at the bottom of the stairs.

My hand grasps the railing, and I realize I'm taking shallow breaths as I climb the stairs. My mind is picturing Chris, shirtless, singing and painting two nights before. I won't let myself wonder why he's so good to a stranger and her baby.

I need this.

I deserve this.

Addy deserves this.

I turn the doorknob and peek inside the room. He didn't just paint the room—which is now a warm candlelight ivory—there's a wall, too, dividing the far third of the room from the rest. It runs halfway across, enough for a private area.

I hurry and look beyond the wall. A double bed and dresser have been set up for me. I have a real bed, not just a mattress on the floor. There's a frame, a box spring, a headboard—it's all there. It's dizzying, seriously dizzying. Who is this boy and how can he be so generous?

It takes me fifteen minutes to drag everything up the steps. Then I carry Addy up and lay her in her Pack 'n Play while I unpack our new towels and wonder where the bathroom is. Since Addy's still content and nobody's home to show me around, I go downstairs to snoop.

At the bottom of the stairs, the family room and front door are to my right, and the kitchen is to my left. The kitchen is bright with white cupboards. A long oak table sits in the middle with six chairs. Two are mismatched. There's a lazy Susan in the middle of the table holding salt and pepper shakers and napkins. There's a sticky ring on the table at the seat on the end.

I'm biting my lip. My heart is about to slip up my throat. Other than the ring on the table, there's no grease or grime anywhere. All the cupboard doors are intact, closed, and on hinges.

I open the fridge. It's not full, but there's milk . . . and orange juice . . . cheese, lunch meat, and some leftovers in a plastic container—spaghetti, maybe. Real people live here, not like at my house. At my house, we're dead; we just keep breathing and keep waking up waiting for it to be over. But here they're alive—for real.

A toaster sits in the middle of the counter with a plate beside it and a tub of butter. Crumbs litter the plate and countertop. Breakfast before work—what a concept.

I grab a dishcloth from the sink and wipe the table and counters. I push the toaster back against the wall, then put the plate in the sink and the butter in the refrigerator.

These men need someone to take care of them. God knows it can't be me, but I can do my part to help while I struggle to keep Addy and myself fed, and with a roof over us.

There's a back door at the far right end of the kitchen. Through the square window in the door, I can see that it leads out to the patio. On the far left of the kitchen is a small hallway with a laundry room off of it.

I traipse into the family room and down the hallway that runs alongside the staircase. There are two bedrooms and a bathroom at the back of the house. I stop and close my eyes, breathing in Chris's scent.

Without thinking, I walk into the first bedroom on the left. His guitar is lying on his bed, on top of a navy blue comforter, hastily yanked up but still messy. He has a Spiderman pillowcase, and seeing it makes me happy for some reason. I run my hand over it and smile.

Three beat-up, broken guitars lean against the far wall, under a window. On a shelf above the bed, there's a collection of superhero bobbleheads. I tap each one and crack up watching them bounce on spring necks. They're dusty. I wonder how long he's had them.

A well-worn houndstooth newsboy cap hangs off of his computer monitor. Next to it, empty Coke cans are stacked in a pyramid—their precise spacing an oddity in this disaster of a bedroom.

There's a dresser with its drawers pulled out, overflowing

with unfolded jeans and T-shirts, and a pile of clothes on the floor in front of the closet. Black Converse high-tops peek out from beneath the jumble of clothes.

My hand reaches for a T-shirt, but I pull it back.

I'm a creeper.

I shake my head, returning to my senses. Addy starts crying upstairs.

By four o'clock, I'm bored out of my mind. Addy's been fed, and I've eaten half a pack of M&M's I found in the bottom of my bag. I can recite every nonperishable food item in the kitchen cupboards and list the reading material on the floor beside Chris's bed: Steven Tyler's rock-and-roll memoir, the book *World War Z*, and several Marvel comics.

I load Addy up in her stroller, determined to find a park or somewhere to waste time during my days until I find a job. We head down the sidewalk, over the cracks and bumps made by the tree roots that have grown too big over the years.

Dappled sunlight filters through the green leaves above us. Addy squints and jerks her head every time the sun shines through the branches into her stroller.

I'm surprised to find people out in their yards at this time of day. There seem to be a lot of stay-at-home moms watching their kids play around, and retired people mowing well-watered, emerald-green lawns.

This is nothing like where I'm from.

This is how normal people live.

People with real jobs.

People who don't sell drugs or sex or babies.

A little boy dashes down his driveway toward us, on a small black and silver bike with training wheels. He's not stopping. Immediately, I realize he doesn't know how to stop. He's screaming, and his mom's running after him.

I push the stroller out of the way and prepare to catch him or be hit. The front tire of the little bike smashes into my bare leg as my hands grasp the handlebars. "Got ya!"

Pain sears through my shin. Blood's dripping down into my sock.

"Oh my gosh!" The mom grabs her son, squeezing him to her chest, while her eyes examine my leg. "Come on." She motions for me to follow her as she rushes back up the driveway. "I'll get some Band-Aids."

I tug the stroller along behind me, following the woman and little boy up the driveway to the open garage. "I'll just wait. . . ."

She's already inside. I can hear her scolding her son. "I told you not to touch that bike until I was done bringing the groceries inside and could watch you!"

Addy's kicking and squirming in her stroller, and I'm afraid she's about to have a fit. The woman bursts back through the door and walks through the garage to where I'm standing.

"I'm so sorry about that." She hands me a wet paper towel and some Band-Aids. "He's not quite five and doesn't know how to ride it very well yet."

"That's okay." I wipe my leg and apply the bandages. "It's not that bad. I'm glad I was there to run into." I laugh, trying to make her concerned expression fade. "He might have ended up worse than me."

"No doubt he would have. He's an accident waiting to happen. Thanks for catching him." She chuckles and shakes her head. "I'm Gail." She reaches out and shakes my hand.

"Fai—" I cough, covering up my near-blunder. "Leah."

She looks down at Addy. "What a beautiful baby."

"Thanks." I brush Addy's wispy hair back. "Her name's Addy."

"Where do you live? I haven't seen you around here before."

Her little boy comes back out and begins to stomp through the flower bed. I point down the street toward the white cape cod with the black shutters and green awnings.

"We just moved in down the street."

She follows my finger and her eyes widen. "With Ken Buckridge?" Then she peers down at Addy again. "Oh. I didn't know Chris had a girlfriend."

"No! No, I'm not." I indicate Addy. "She's not. I'm only renting their upstairs. We just met yesterday."

Gail smiles, but the corners of her mouth are tight, and there are creases between her eyebrows. "I didn't know they were renting the upstairs." She squeezes Addy's teeny foot, and her jaw quirks, relaxes. "You two will be good for them."

I have no idea what she's talking about, but my leg's throbbing and starting to swell, and I just want to sit down. "Well, it was nice meeting you. I think Addy's going to start fussing soon, so I'm going to get her back home."

"Okay, well, stop by and visit sometime. I'll introduce you to some of the other women in the neighborhood."

"That sounds nice." I give the stroller a nudge and try not to limp as we head back down to the sidewalk. I wave and smile, attempting to hide the pain I'm in. "Bye."

Halfway to 356 Maple, I see a black pickup truck pulls into the driveway. Music blares from the open windows. Chris's hair blows around in the breeze.

My heart jumps to life.

How have I become so hooked on a guy I met yesterday? But watching him park his truck and hop out, I know how.

Nobody's ever done half as much for me, and he doesn't even know me. He's a good person, and I haven't known many of those.

On his way to the front door, he stops when he spots us. "Hey!" His smile's genuine and fills his whole face. He jogs across the yard to meet us.

After seeing his room, I half expect him to be wearing a superhero T-shirt, but he just has on a plain white T-shirt covered in dirt. He's filthy. "All moved in?" he asks.

"Yeah." I watch his tall frame moving toward me, his jeans shifting with each stride, his shirt hugging his chest. I stop the stroller as he reaches us. "I love the paint color and the privacy wall. Thanks."

He bends down, leaning his head into the stroller. His fingers wrap lightly around Addy's arm. "You're welcome. Listen, I'm really sorry about what happened. My dad can be . . . I don't know what's wrong with him sometimes. Do you need help moving anything in?"

I ignore the jab in the pit of my stomach at the mention of Chris's dad. "No, we're good. We don't have much, so it wasn't difficult."

He unbuckles Addy and lifts her out of the stroller. "Is it okay if I carry her in?"

I cringe at the dirt on his shirt, but he's already got her pressed against his chest. "Sure." I can always give her a bath.

She turns her head toward his neck and snuggles into a ball. Somehow she feels how I do with him.

Safe.

Secure.

Home.

All those months inside my mother must've made her feel unloved, unwanted, adrift. Now she has me to take care of her, and Chris, too, I guess. It's a mystery what he's providing her with—us with—but whatever he's offering, we're taking it.

I follow behind him, pushing the stroller alongside Mom's car, which makes my stomach lurch. I have to do something about those Ohio plates. Will they even be looking for a stolen car from Ohio in Florida? I don't know, but I can't chance it.

At the front steps, Chris hands Addy over to me, takes the stroller, and begins to fold it up. I wonder at his stroller expertise—since I almost lost my mind trying to figure it out.

"What happened to your leg?"

I look down at my bandages and shrug. "Oh, nothing really. Just saved the life of the little boy down the street. You know, nothing big."

He lifts his eyebrows and laughs. "What? The little hellion who lives in the Tudor?" He points to Gail's house.

"Yeah. He doesn't quite have the hang of using the brakes on his bike."

Chris carries the stroller inside. "Heroics always make me hungry. How about you?" He sets the stroller at the bottom of the stairs. "I'm craving pizza. Want some?"

Pizza sounds amazing. "Definitely."

"Cool, I'll order. What do you like on it?"

"Anything's fine with me. Just no anchovies." I curl my lip at the thought of salty, crispy fish mingling with my cheese and pepperoni. I used to despise touching them at Giovanni's.

Chris laughs and puts a cell phone to his ear. I head toward the stairs while he's ordering.

"Don't touch that stroller," he says, cupping the phone. "I'll get it."

My leg throbs with each step I take, and I'm relieved when I'm finally sitting on my blue couch.

With Addy on my lap, sucking on her pacifier, I try to talk myself into getting up now to make a bottle, instead of waiting until my leg is black and purple and twice the size it should be. I slide to the edge of the couch cushion and am just up on my feet again when I hear a siren blaring down the street.

A cop cruiser.

chapter

nine

I forget about my leg. Addy's left lying on the couch. My hands grab everything they can reach—bottles, formula, diapers—and shove it all into the diaper bag.

I'm desperately trying to collapse Addy's Pack 'n Play, but one side is stuck. Shoving and kicking it isn't helping. "Come on!" I kick it again.

"Making a quick getaway?"

I spin. My heart feels like it's just been kicked instead of the stupid Pack 'n Play. Chris sets the stroller on the floor by the door, and a confused expression crosses his face.

What am I going to tell him?

It's quiet.

There's no siren.

I dart to the window and look out, expecting the cop car to be parked in his driveway or out front on the street. But it's nowhere in sight.

I bite my lip and feel my shoulders shrink in on themselves as I turn to face him. "No, just . . . um . . ."

He shakes his head. "It's cool. You can ask me for help, you know. We'll move it into your bedroom after I shower. Pizza will be here in forty."

He turns and is gone, back down the stairs, and I'm standing at the window feeling like a total idiot. Judging from the bewildered look on his face, he knew I wasn't having trouble trying to move the Pack 'n Play a whole ten feet into my bedroom. But whatever he really thought, he covered for me so I wouldn't be embarrassed.

Addy's voice starts out low, then reaches much higher decibels. At least she's a distraction. I rush to make her bottle and settle back on the couch to feed her, grabbing a dirty T-shirt back out from the diaper bag, where I'd just stuffed it. With the puke-stained shirt over my shoulder, I give her the bottle and let her drink.

She's so warm and relaxing, the weight of her in my arm, her steady breathing, the squeaky *sucksucksuck* sound of the nipple while she's eating. I rest my head against the cushions on the back of the sofa. My eyelids feel heavy, like they're weighed down. I can hardly keep them open.

The doorbell startles me. My eyelids fly open. Addy jolts, and her eyes pop open too. I lift her, and she pukes. Big shock. I sigh and pat her back, making sure she's okay.

I stand, and her bottle rolls off my lap and onto the floor. Back behind the wall, in my bedroom, I lay Addy on my bed and change her diaper before changing my shirt. By the time I'm cleaned up, she's asleep, and I put her down in her Pack 'n Play.

There's a knock on my door. It's Chris. Who else would it be? He smells like soap, and he's changed out of his dirty work clothes into basketball shorts and a T-shirt.

He has a pizza box in one hand, and a six-pack of Coke in the other. "Want to eat up here or downstairs?" He glances down at the box. "Or you can just take your half if you want. I shouldn't assume—"

"No. I'll eat with you." I push my hair back behind my ear. "Downstairs, I guess. Addy's asleep." I nod toward the Pack 'n Play. "I don't want to wake her. I'll just leave the door up here open in case she wakes up."

We tread lightly down the stairs and into the living room. He sits on the couch, and I sit on the floor, the coffee table between us. He pulls a Coke free and hands it to me. "Guess I should get some plates."

I jump up, and my leg stings. I cringe. "Paper towels will work. I'll grab them." As I'm retrieving the paper towels from the kitchen, I hear the TV come on. I set the roll on the coffee table and lower myself back down to the carpet, pushing my hair behind both ears, careful with my leg.

He hasn't looked at me since we came downstairs. His eyes are glued to the TV. The awkwardness is growing with each passing second. I can't let him think he has some freak living upstairs. "Look, about earlier—"

"Really," he says, cutting me off, "I don't need to know. It's cool." He takes a bite of pizza.

"It's just—"

He holds up a hand and shakes his head, chewing.

"I don't want you to think I'm weird."

His eyes finally meet mine and he's laughing. "Why would I think that? Because you were fighting with a Pack 'n Play?"

"Well . . . yeah." I shrug. My hair falls into my face, and I tuck it behind my ear again.

He shakes his head and rolls his eyes. "Just eat your pizza." He pulls the box open and gestures for me to grab a piece.

I take one and pull it out. Long strings of cheese hold on to the other pieces, and I swipe them with my finger, tearing them apart. I take a bite. It's the best pizza I've ever tasted. I'm used to my pizza at home, and this makes Giovanni's taste like crap.

Everything back home was crap.

After a few minutes of Chris flipping through the channels with the remote while we eat, I have to break the silence again. "How was work? Where do you work, anyway?"

"I have a glamorous job roofing houses for RJ Roofing." He leans back and rubs his stomach. "I've been there a couple of years. It's not bad. They're good people to work for."

"That sounds horrible to me."

He lifts one eyebrow.

"I'm terrified of heights. I couldn't ever go up on a roof. Plus, it has to be about a hundred and fifty degrees up there."

He chuckles. "It is. And you come home covered in tar and dirt. But the pay's good."

We both eat another piece of pizza and stare at the TV.

"How long have you played the guitar?"

I hate that he won't ask me his own questions even if I won't answer them anyway.

He stretches both arms over his head and yawns. "About five years."

I nod and tuck my hair back again.

"Here." He reaches into his pocket and shoots me with a rubber band. "For your hair. It's not going to stay behind your ears." His smile's easy.

Tonight, his eyes match his dark blue shirt. I like his chin-length hair down. It makes the angles of his face softer. Faint stubble has grown on his chin. No wonder I'm obsessed with him. He's hot.

My eyes make their way back to his, and I can tell he

knows what I'm thinking. I shift to peer at the TV, feeling my pulse race. I ball my hair on top of my head and wrap the band around it.

"Faith," he mumbles.

I jerk around. "What did you say?"

"The tattoo on the back of your neck, it says 'hope and faith.' "

I reach around with my hand, covering my tattoo. It's a banner inside angel wings with our names on it. Hope and Faith. My sister and I got them last summer. It took me forever and five days to talk her into it. She got hers as a tramp stamp, thinking she could hide it. More people have seen hers than mine, though, since her track pants sit low on her hips.

"Yeah." I swallow my fight-or-flight instinct. "Do you have any tattoos?"

In one swift movement, he whips off his T-shirt. There, in the middle of his tan chest, beside a smear of paint, is a cross with two dates inscribed on it. One across, one down. Its intricate design has my fingers itching to touch. Instead, I crawl on my knees around the table to get a closer look.

I want to ask the significance of the dates, but it feels way too personal to ask.

When I'm finished ogling, he pulls his T-shirt back on. "You're not the only one with secrets." Before I can say anything, he's standing and collecting the pizza box, paper towels, and Coke cans.

"Here, let me help." I take the cans and sauce-stained paper towels and follow him out to the kitchen. He opens the patio door and takes the pizza box outside.

Figuring there's a trash can out there that he's headed to, I go with him. After we toss our trash, he plops down at the patio table. There's a small in-ground pool in the back yard that I can't keep my eyes off of.

"It's a nice night," he says. "You should go for a swim."

I motion toward the house. "Addy. I should probably go back in so I can hear her."

He pulls at the skin under his chin and stands. "I'll go check on her, if it's okay?" he asks.

"Yeah. Okay. I'll go too."

He leads the way back inside, up the steps, and through my door. I peer into the Pack 'n Play. "She's still asleep."

Chris creeps over and studies her. He watches for a few minutes, then turns back and stops, catching my confused expression.

Then he smiles and continues past me, out into the living area.

He might be as weird as me.

Before he sits on the couch, he picks up Addy's bottle that fell onto the floor earlier, then tosses it to me. "Good catch," he says when I grab it out of the air.

As I'm rinsing the bottle in the sink, he starts humming and tapping his fingers on the arm of the couch.

"What song is that?" I ask. "I don't recognize it."

"It's mine. My band's rehearsing it tonight. I think we'll debut it on Saturday. We've got a gig in Jacksonville."

I've always been a sucker for musicians, not that I've ever dated one. I've only dated Jason, the delivery guy, and he couldn't sing his way out of a pizza box, let alone play an instrument. "Can I hear it?"

His face lights up like a kid at Christmas. This was a setup—he wanted me to ask. That's why he started humming. I wonder what else he could get me to fall for.

He nods toward the stairs. "Come down and I'll play it."

He leads me out the door. "Don't forget to leave that open."

"You're a better parent than me," I mutter. He doesn't hear me. He's halfway down the stairs, too excited about showing off his guitar playing.

I follow him down the hall to where I already know his bedroom is because I'm a snoop. I stand in the doorway while he piles clothes into his drawers and attempts to shove them closed. Then he yanks his blanket up over his pillow, hiding Spidey.

He runs his palms down his shorts and picks up his guitar. I slide in and sit on the edge of his bed. He sits next to me.

"Nice bobbleheads," I say, my lips twitching.

"Are you making fun of my vintage Spiderman and Superman?" He gets up on his knees and taps their heads like I did earlier. I panic, wondering if I left fingerprints. If so, he doesn't seem to notice. "I've had them since I was little."

"Oh, you don't still collect superhero stuff, though?"

He turns to me, smiling a crooked smile. A dimple dents his right cheek. "Okay. Maybe I still have a thing for super-heroes." He holds up his hand with his finger and thumb so close together, there's barely any space between them. "This much."

The mattress bounces as he plops back down beside me. My eyes slip over his room as he picks up his guitar. He follows my gaze. Then he gets up and snags the houndstooth cap off of the corner of his monitor and puts it on his head backward. "This was my grandpa Buckridge's cap. I wear it mostly when I play. He was the one who taught me."

He sits back down, and I feel like I'm breathing way too loud, like I'm gasping to get enough air and my chest is heaving. He's so . . . normal, with his grandpa's cap and superhero collection. I've never had a collection of anything. There was no money for food, let alone ceramic ponies or sparkly unicorns. Hell, our electric got shut off at least three times a year.

I remember once when Hope and I were little and we dug all the beer-bottle caps out of the trash and colored them with markers. We pretended they were magic coins for a pretend land, and if we found the entrance and deposited the coins, we could get in. Sometimes I still want to search for our pretend land.

I watch Chris's fingers work the strings, and when he starts singing, the room, my mind, my entire being, are filled with his voice. He's so close, I can almost feel his breath on my ear. Thinking of the sensation that would bring sends chills down the back of my neck.

He shifts, and our legs touch. Mine scraped and bruised from the kid down the street, his strong and tan.

When he stops playing, Addy's cries echo through the house. We both look at each other. We couldn't hear her over his guitar.

I spring up. "Thanks for playing for me. I love it. Seriously, it's great." I dart out of his room, down the hallway, and up the stairs to Addy. I pick her up out of the Pack 'n Play and bounce her a little bit. "Shh . . . it's okay, sweet pea." I turn around, rocking her in my arms, and bump right into Chris.

"Maybe she wants this," he says, holding up her pacifier. "It was on your couch."

"Thanks." I take it from him, wondering if I have a second shadow now, and rinse it in the sink.

I'm not sure how I feel about this. I like him. I think I like him a lot. I wouldn't stop him if he ever tried to kiss me, that's for damn sure.

"Well, I'll leave you two alone." He runs his fingers through the back of his hair. He's waiting for me to ask him to stay. Maybe I should.

Before I decide, he's out the door.

"Good night!" I call after him.

It hits me that I didn't pay him for my half of the pizza. Back in my bedroom, in my top dresser drawer, I pull a ten-dollar bill loose from a stack of money I stashed with my underwear.

As I bound down the stairs, Addy's pacifier pops out of her mouth and bounces down to the last step. She starts to whimper.

"Hey, Leah? You need me?" Chris's feet pad down the hallway toward us.

"Just . . ." I juggle Addy to my other shoulder, stepping to the bottom of the stairs as he rounds the corner. I dig in my pocket for the ten. "I have money. . . ." Her whine escalates into a full-out screech. I yank my hand out of my pocket before finding the ten and kneel to pick up the pacifier at the same time Chris bends to retrieve it.

Our heads bash together. "Shit," I hiss, rubbing my forehead.

Chris's face twists into a grimace. He rubs his forehead too, with the pacifier hooked around one finger. "Got it."

He hands me the pacifier, and we both bust out laughing. Soon we're in hysterics, rubbing our heads. I sit back on the bottom step and push the pacifier in Addy's mouth to stop her howling. "I'm sorry!" My stomach aches from laughing so hard.

"It wasn't your fault." He's on his knees in front of me. "I think I have a concussion. Your head's like a freakin' bowling ball." His laugh's deep and contagious.

I double over, cracking up. Even though I'm still holding

Addy tight, she's squirming and doing the scared thing with her arms shooting out, but I can't help it. The look on his face—his lip cocked up in a lopsided grin, his brows raised above teasing blue eyes—is so funny, I can't stop laughing.

"I need some ice," he says, and eases up off the floor. "I'm already getting a big knot on my head."

After a couple of deep, steadying breaths, I stand too. "I'll get it for you. It was my bowling-ball head that caused this, after all." I hold Addy out for him to take. "Can you hold her?"

He takes Addy in his arms. "It's not your fault, and your head's not any harder than mine. I was just kidding." He's still smiling, and I feel warm all over.

The back door swings open, and a man comes bustling in with two plastic grocery bags. His hair is black, but his angular profile is identical to Chris's. "Chris, I'm—" He freezes.

Chris tucks Addy into my arms. "Hey, Dad. This is Leah. The girl upstairs."

Chris's dad's eyes shift from his son to me. He nods and sets the grocery bags on the counter. "Nice to meet you, Leah, I'm Ken Buckridge."

"Nice to meet you, Mr. Buckridge. Thank you for renting your upstairs to me and Addy." I hold her a little tighter and rest my chin on top of her head.

"I didn't realize you had an infant yesterday. I'm sorry for the . . . uh . . . miscommunication." The muscles in his jaw work as he takes in the baby. "How old?"

"Two months." I try to think back, hoping that's the age I told Ivy. "Is it okay? The baby being here?"

Chris grabs my arm, claiming my attention. "Of course it's okay. Why wouldn't it be?" He snorts, like this is the dumbest thought a person could have, and shakes his head. "I'll bring you some ice upstairs."

When he drops his hand, I turn back to the steps. Out of the corner of my eye, I see Mr. Buckridge watching Chris and me, concern smudged across his face. I make my way, rapidly, up the stairs. The easy comfort I found with Chris has been replaced by the taunting feeling that Addy and I aren't welcome. It's clear Mr. Buckridge doesn't want us here.

chapter

ten

Chris and I sit on my couch, plastic bags of melted ice in our laps. He's slouched down with his head resting on the back of the cushions and his long legs stretched out in front of him. I'm curled up with my legs underneath me.

It's comfortable and strange at the same time. He feels like my new best friend who I've only known for forty-eight hours. He's all I have now—him and Addy—and it scares the hell out of me. If I've learned anything in the past sixteen years, it's that I can't depend on anyone, let alone someone I just met, even if I want to.

I miss Hope so badly, it feels like someone's ripping my heart into tiny pieces inside my chest. She always knows who to trust. Like Brian. Somehow, even though he was the guy all the girls threw themselves at, she knew he wasn't a player and she could trust him. She also told me that Jason wanted only one thing. I wonder what she'd think about Chris?

God, what Hope must think of me. She already thinks I'm stupid. I know that she would think I'm a complete freaking idiot for doing this.

And she'd be right.

I can just see the look on her face when Mom told her I took Addy and bolted. That tilted eyebrow, lips parted, disgusted look. This time with a little bit of regret underneath. Regret that she hadn't known and hadn't been able to stop me, and regret that she was never brave enough to do something this ballsy.

"What are you thinking about?"

Chris's question jolts me back to the present. "Nothing, why?"

"You're picking at your Band-Aid, and your forehead's all scrunched up."

"Your dad doesn't want Addy here, does he?" I have no idea where that came from. I mean, I hadn't been thinking it, but out it comes.

Chris lays his hand over mine to stop my persistent picking, and I snatch my arm away. "Sorry," he mumbles, and tilts his head away from mine.

I feel like a jerk. "It's okay." I wish I'd kept my hand under his, but instinct makes me pull back. It's my flipping mother's fault. My ex-boyfriend, Jason, was right. I'm sexually scarred for life because of her. Maybe if I hadn't grown up watching her with different guys spending the night all the time, I'd be normal.

"Of course my dad wants Addy here," Chris says, ignoring the awkwardness between us. "Why wouldn't he? What kind of evil bastard doesn't like babies?" He cracks a smile, but it doesn't look genuine.

"He looked at her like she was his personal demon."

Something about Chris's expression gives me affirmation, but he says, "It's okay."

"It's not okay. It sucks."

He chuckles, trying to break the tension, and stretches back out, leaning his head toward mine again. "Guess I can't go to band practice with a concussion. You need a TV up here, Bowling-Ball Head."

"Yeah, it's on my wish list."

"I think we have an old one in the basement. I'll go down in the morning and bring it up." He yawns and stretches both arms above his head. "I'm heading downstairs." He sits up straight on the edge of the couch and squeezes my shoulder. "Sweet dreams." His sleepy blue-green eyes blink, then he rubs them and stands.

I watch his easy stride as he crosses the room to the door. "Night." I close my eyes, not wanting to see him disappear down the stairs, and listen as the door clicks shut behind him.

This is so bad. So freaking bad. It's two in the morning. Addy woke up for a bottle, I gave it to her, she spewed it all over, and now she's clutching her chest like she's in pain.

I tread back and forth through the kitchen area, into my bedroom, back into the living area. I bounce on my toes and pat her back as she shrieks at the top of her tiny lungs.

My leg's a swollen, throbbing mess.

I try to stuff her pacifier in her mouth and hold it there, but she's not having it. She wants everyone on the block to know how pissed she is and how much she's hurting. I'm about to join her. Screaming my brains out is the only option I have left.

The knock is soft. I barely hear it before the door opens

and Chris is peering through the crack. I motion for him to come in.

"I don't know what the hell's wrong with her. She keeps grabbing at her chest." I run a hand through my hair, suddenly aware of how shitty I look in my tattered cotton shorts and horrifically embarrassed that I'm wearing his T-shirt that I borrowed the other day. If God has plans for me to die young, now would be the perfect time.

"Let me try." He holds out his hands, and I pass Addy to him. He also takes her pacifier. "Shh . . . ," he says as he bounces, rocks, and begins to walk my path.

Addy stops raging and cries at a normal decibel level, blinking her eyes, curious about being handed off. Chris takes the opportunity to stick the pacifier back in her mouth. He disappears into my bedroom with her.

Fifteen minutes pass, and I'm falling asleep on the couch, leaning on my hand. It strikes me that the constant stream of baby cries has ceased. I wander into the bedroom and find Chris on my bed, asleep on his back, with Addy dozing on his chest.

The weirdest feeling comes over me, and I can't tear my eyes from them, so peaceful, so perfect together. They were meant to be. Whatever happens, they have to stay together.

I've never had an urge as strong as the one to crawl into bed beside them and curl up next to Chris. Instead, I lift the second pillow from my bed and head out to the couch, but I can't stop thinking of him.

When I wake the next morning, Chris is gone. There's a TV on my end table hooked up and ready to go, and Addy's asleep in her Pack 'n Play, which has been moved into my bedroom.

Again, I wonder why he's taken us under his wing, what

he's getting out of it. There has to be something. Nobody's that nice without a motive.

There's a stabbing pain in my neck from sleeping in an awkward position, and my leg is still pounding. My bladder's about to burst, so I tiptoe downstairs, wondering if Mr. Buckridge is home and awake, wishing I had a bathroom upstairs.

There's no sign of him, and I make it unnoticed to the bathroom. When I come back out, though, he's in the kitchen making coffee and spins around when he hears me reach the stairs.

For a second, we just stare at each other. Then I smile. "Good morning, Mr. Buckridge."

"Morning, Leah. Sleep well?" He turns back around and pours coffee grounds into the filter.

"Great, thanks." I jog up the stairs and realize my underarms are damp. I hope I get used to Chris's dad fast. I don't want to be a nervous wreck all the time.

I peek in on Addy again, and for a minute I watch her sleep. Both arms are in the air, hands in fists by her head. Her knees are bent and fall to the sides. Even though she's only been alive a few days, she looks different, bigger. Or maybe I'm just used to her now.

It's a miracle that nothing's wrong with her. She doesn't shake like a baby drug addict going through detox. That's a bonus. I guess she's healthy. I hope I can keep her that way.

My fingers trail along the purple lace on her romper. Being with her makes me breathe more evenly, makes my eyes focus, calms my insides. She's an anchor, even if I have no clue what to do with her, or how to make her happy.

There's no way I should have a baby.

After Addy wakes up and I give her a bottle and eat a bowl

of cereal, we attempt to find the park again. Hopefully this time neither one of us will be hit by a kid on a runaway two-wheeler. On the way back, I want to take the long way home so I can pick up job applications from any places that look halfway promising.

Gail's fixing her trampled flower garden when we walk by her house. "Hey!" she calls, waving. "Leah! Come have coffee. Can you stay a few minutes?"

Ugh. I just want to get this kid to the park. That's why we're in this town—good schools, sidewalks, parks. *Job.* Can't forget my lack of cash and the applications waiting to be picked up and filled out.

On the other hand, maybe Gail knows where I can get a job. "Sure, we have a few minutes." I smile, pushing Addy's stroller up Gail's driveway.

She tucks stray hairs back into the red bandanna tied around her head and wipes her cheek, leaving a smear of dirt. "How's your leg?" When she sees it, she sucks air in through her teeth. "Ouch, that looks sore."

"It's okay. I'll live."

She laughs. "Good. I don't need to be sued. I can barely afford this house as it is." Holding up one finger for me to wait, she peeks around the side of the house. "Jonathan, I'm going inside! Stay in the backyard."

I unbuckle Addy and pick her up, then follow Gail through her garage. She shucks her gardening gloves as we're walking and drops them on the roof of her burgundy Grand Am. "It's too hot to be outside. I've got the AC on. We'll sit in the family room and chat."

Her house is spotless. The parquet floor under my feet shines with polish, the beige carpet in the family room has vacuum tracks through it. Candles and dried flower arrangements are set in the center of dark oak tables, and it smells like magnolias.

"Do you take cream and sugar? I have some Sweet'N Low, or flavored creamer."

"Just black, please." She crinkles her nose, but I've grown accustomed to the bitter taste. Coffee was a staple in our house. Milk was not. Sweet'N Low, no way—the only white powder that made it into our house was snortable.

From the family room, I watch Gail in the kitchen pouring coffee. She comes back to where I'm standing and sets the mugs on coasters on the flawless wood surface of her coffee table. Then she sits down on the ivory couch. I sit next to her, too nervous to pick up my coffee for fear I'll spill some in her immaculate ivory and beige room, or worse yet, on Addy.

She's lying cradled in my left arm, her big grayish blue eyes transfixed on my face. She's so still, it's like she's asleep with her eyes open.

"I was just telling Janine the other night—she lives across the street—that the Buckridges have a renter. A young girl." She pats my leg. "With a *baby*!" she coos and shakes Addy's foot.

Addy grunts, not happy to be bothered.

"Yeah." I smile, wondering what to say to that, and why it makes her so giddy that I'm a young girl, with a *baby*!

"So, what are your plans? Are you job hunting?"

"I am job hunting. Do you know of any place that's hiring? I'll do anything; I just need cash."

"Hmm . . ." She twists her lips and scrunches her eyebrows as she thinks. The doorbell rings, and Gail looks annoyed. "Hold that thought."

I clench my fist. I need help with this whole job thing.

A second female voice echoes through the front hallway,

and then two sets of footsteps are coming back. Make that three, as a tiny blond girl scuffs her tennis shoes on the carpet, stopping when she sees me. She reminds me of Hope when we were little.

Behind her, Gail and the lady, who I'm guessing is the little girl's mom, are chattering, and they walk into the kitchen, probably for another cup of coffee.

The little girl puts her hands on her hips, cocks her head, and frowns. "That's not your baby."

I'd laugh if I weren't about to choke. I force a smile. "Of course it is. Would you like to see her?" I hold Addy out, showing her to the little girl.

"You're not old enough to have a baby. My daddy says you have to be thirty and married and have a nice house before the stork will let you have one. I tried asking Santa for one, but he just brought me a fake one instead. I cut all her hair off and had to sit in the corner for five minutes. Then—"

"Emma, go outside and play with Jonathan." The little girl's mom takes her by the shoulders and steers her to the French doors behind the dining table. Now that I look outside, I see the little hellion, as Chris calls him, whacking the picnic table with a gigantic stick. I already know how this will end. The little girl will be inside crying her brains out in ten minutes—if that long.

Gail breezes back into the room and places a third mug of coffee on a coaster. "This is Janine Evans from across the street—who I was telling you about. And Emma. She's seven." She shakes her head and whispers, "And quite a handful." Then she tugs a chair over from the dining table so Janine can sit and reach her coffee. "Janine, this is Leah."

"Nice to meet you," Janine says, sitting and brushing her wispy blond hair back off her face. It's dry and brittle, and bleached that color. Her capri pants dig into her waist, making a bulge over the top that her white knit shirt clings to.

"Hi." I watch her fan herself with her hand.

"Whew. That kid's gonna kill me someday. It's too hot for coffee, Gail. Got iced tea?"

"Sun tea's brewing outside on the picnic table."

I peer out, wondering if the tea pitcher has fallen victim to the hellion's big stick.

"Can I hold your baby?" Janine asks. "I wish Emma was still that size. They grow so fast."

Addy's still calm, taking it all in. I almost say no, afraid to chance a baby mood swing, but hand her over anyway. Janine beams and cuddles Addy into her chest. "Gail says you're staying at Ken Buckridge's house." She lifts her eyes to Gail, and a look passes between them.

I don't know what the look means.

"Yeah." I shift and put my hands under my thighs. I really just want to go to the park.

"Ken's a nice man, don't you think, Gail?"

Gail sputters, then coughs. Coffee sprays everywhere. "Wrong pipe," she says, straining through her coughing fit.

"I'll get you some water." Happy to have an escape from the Weird Sisters, I jump up and dash into the kitchen. After opening two cupboards, I find the glasses and fill one with water.

Gail's still coughing when I return, but not as much. She mutters "thank you" when I hand her the glass.

Janine bounces Addy on her knee like she's two years old, and not two months, which she isn't anyway. Addy's head is bobbling around.

"I think we're going to get going. It's about time for another bottle, and I don't have one with me." I grab Addy off of Janine's lap and head for the door to the garage before either of them can stop me. "Thanks for the coffee," I say, shoving my way out the door.

Outside, I take a huge gulp of air and hold it in for ten seconds, then push it out. "That was painful, huh?"

Addy squirms and lets out a sharp shriek.

"Yeah, I could scream too. Let's go to the park now. Hope you don't mind if I grab a few applications on our way home. You like wearing diapers and eating, don't you?"

She kicks and waves her fists.

"That's what I thought."

chapter

eleven

When we get back late in the afternoon, there's a car in our driveway that I've never seen. Chris and Mr. Buckridge aren't home, and I instantly feel like throwing up, wondering if the person inside is waiting to arrest me and take Addy back.

Then logic sets in. Whoever it is has to have a key. Anyone here to arrest me wouldn't be inside.

Unless that person has a warrant.

Shit. I don't know what to do. They're blocking my car. I don't have the car keys anyway. Addy's fussy and wants to be out of the heat. I'm screwed.

Without any other options, I push the stroller around to the patio, lift Addy out, and go inside through the back door.

The smells of lemon wood polish and spaghetti sauce fill my nose. There's a plump old lady with curly gray hair stirring a pot on the stove. "Hello!" she trills when she sees me, dropping her spoon and rushing over to kiss my cheek and lift Addy out of my arms. "Christopher told me you had a baby. I'm his grandma, Ken's mom. I come over most days to take care of my boys, clean, you know, things like that." She squeezes Addy tight. "Aren't you just the smallest little bundle ever? Little sweetie. Grandma will love you up!" She makes her way by the table, her hips bumping against the chairs as she passes them, and into the family room.

Everything inside me wants to jump for joy. She's not here to arrest me, and I've never had a grandma. I want her to squeeze me and love me up too. I was always jealous of the other kids for having grammies, mee maws, nanas, and grannies.

My mom's mom abandoned her when she was young. I don't blame her. Mom was probably evil then, too.

"Leah, dear?" Mrs. Buckridge calls from the family room. "I think your little darling needs a diaper. Mind if I go up and change her?"

Do I mind? Hell no. She can change diapers until her fingers fall off. "No, I don't mind. I'll come up with you."

She takes the stairs slowly, planting her feet deliberately on each step, her hand grasping the railing and sliding up as she rises. At the top, she opens the door and goes inside, with me behind her.

"Okay, little darlin', we're going to get you all cleaned up." Her body rocks back and forth as she walks straight into my bedroom. "Diapers in here, Leah?"

"Yeah, on the changing table on the side of the Pack 'n Play." I hurry in after her.

"The things they have for you young moms. Pack 'n Play." She shakes her head, tearing the tabs back on Addy's diaper. "We just tossed a towel on the sofa when we changed our babies, and put them to sleep in a crib."

My eyes snag on Addy's umbilical cord. At two months,

her stub would be gone. At least that's what the baby books I skimmed through told me. Mrs. Buckridge's head tilts. I can tell she's examining it and thinking the same thing.

"I'll get her a crib," I blurt, trying to get her mind off of Addy's belly button and back to our conversation. My hands wring together. I'm screwed. She knows something's up.

She watches me carefully. "It's fine, dear." Her hands rest over mine and squeeze. "You're doing a good job with her. Chris thinks so too. He won't stop talking about the two of you."

I blink a few times. We stare at each other. "Thanks." I'm not sure what to say. Maybe she didn't wonder about Addy's stub. And Chris talks about us? To his grandma? I'm baffled.

Mrs. Buckridge snaps Addy's romper back up. "Get me a bottle and we'll put her down for a nap. She's tired."

This woman's like the baby whisperer or something. How does she know she's tired? She's not crying. I cross to the kitchen area and make a bottle. Mrs. B sits on the couch with Addy. I hand her the bottle and she holds it up, studying it. "She eats this much already? I'm surprised she doesn't throw it all back up."

I'm an idiot. "She does. So, it's too much to give her?"

She lowers the bottle and blinks at me. "Don't those maternity nurses teach new moms anything anymore?" She makes a *tsk tsk* sound while adjusting Addy and slipping the nipple into her mouth. "I'm surprised she takes it all. Guess your eyes are bigger than your stomach," she says to Addy. "Well, I'm not giving you all of it. We'll see how you do with half."

Thank God this woman knows what to do with a baby. Addy's not defective, and she's not going to die. I'm just feeding her until she pukes. Perfect. Nobody on earth is worse at this baby thing than me.

"Can you turn the TV on, Leah? My soap opera's on. Channel eight, please."

I flip the TV to her soap opera and sit on the floor.

"Go on in and take a nap, dear. You look run down. Does the baby keep you up at night?"

I shrug. "She's pretty good. Last night she cried a lot."

"Go." She shoos me with her hand, momentarily taking the bottle from Addy, who squawks in protest. "Go take a nap. We'll be fine."

The bed's cool and soft. I crawl deeper beneath the covers and let them pull me under.

At ten o'clock that night, Addy's asleep and I'm wide awake from napping earlier. Lounging on the couch, I'm trying to fill out applications with the TV chattering in the background. I have one for the gas station down the street, one for McDonald's a block away on the main road, one for a pet store in a strip mall, and one for the Dollar Store where I bought baby wipes today.

It's not like I want any of these jobs, but I can't afford to be picky. I'm not going to get hired anyway, though, because they ask for information I can't put down in writing, like my social security number and the name and phone number of my past employer. One application asks for three professional references.

Seriously? I'm applying to flip burgers, not ensure homeland security. What the hell?

I don't know what I'm going to do with Addy while I work either. Keep her in the car?

I toss the applications off my lap, onto the couch. Anxiety surges through me. I close my eyes and grit my teeth, waiting for it to subside. How can I just pretend that this is my life now? I have no idea what I'm doing.

I want to call Hope. I want her to come get me. I want to be the girl in my photo at the beach with a normal family—with a normal mom. I want to go home to that mom. I want that time back. I want Addy to have that kind of life.

Tears start falling hot and fast from my eyes. A single sob escapes my lips before I clench them tight.

This was my decision.

Now I have a baby and have to deal with it.

Now I'm alone and have to get used to loneliness.

The tears are stubborn, though, and refuse to stop. I don't know how long I sit there crying, but my eyes are puffy and gritty. I've wiped them so much, my vision's blurry from smudged mascara. I sniffle, wishing I had a bathroom with some tissues or toilet paper to blow my nose into.

I stumble off the couch. My head spins as I shuffle my feet toward the kitchenette to grab a paper towel, which is better than my sleeve. I take a big breath, about to start blowing, when there's a single rap on the door, and it's opened.

"Leah?" Chris sees me standing by the sink, all snotty and gross. His eyes go wide. "Are you okay?"

I'm mortified, but I nod and finish wiping my nose. I fold the paper towel and swipe it under my eyes, too, where I'm sure my runny eye makeup has me looking like a zombie. At least I don't have his T-shirt on tonight.

"You don't look okay." He eases the door closed.

I shrug. "I'm okay. Really."

He stuffs his hands into his jeans pockets. "Want to talk about it?"

I shake my head.

He nods. "Okay. That's cool. I just got home from band practice and thought I'd see if you wanted to watch TV or something, but I'll leave you alone since you're . . . uh . . .

okay." He grins and runs a hand through his hair.

"No, stay," I blurt way too quickly. The desperation in my voice makes me cringe.

"You sure?" He raises his eyebrows. His eyes kill me. They're so sincere.

I smile, attempting to bring myself back under control. "Of course." My hand yanks open the fridge door, and I pull out two cans of Coke. "Catch!"

He clasps his hands around the one I toss to him and pops it open. "Thanks. Hey, I'm going to go change. I'll be right back."

He takes a step toward the door, then turns back around. "How's Addy? Can I look in on her?"

"She's great." I motion toward the bedroom and watch as he quietly enters.

I think I'm falling for a guy who's in love with my kidnapped baby. My life is a bad prime-time drama.

chapter

twelve

I love that I have only a couch. Chris has to sit next to me when he comes back up from changing into his basketball shorts and Superman T-shirt—Superman rocking out on a guitar.

My eyes dart from his shirt to his face, and I crack up laughing.

"Shut up," he says with a sheepish smile. "My grandma got it for me for Christmas. I have to wear it."

He grabs the remote off the cushion beside me as he flops down and flips on Letterman. I watch him bend down and set his Coke can on the floor at his feet.

While he's absorbed in the show, I'm kind of staring at him and hoping he doesn't notice. I turned the lights off, so it's dark except for the light flickering from the TV. I shift so that my leg, which is drawn up and bent, brushes his.

I wonder why a guy like him is always hanging out at

home. He has a band, so I'm guessing he has friends. "No big plans tonight?"

He swivels to face me. "Nah, my friends all hang out with their girlfriends unless we have a gig." His gaze falls down over my chest, up to my eyes, then he shrugs.

I'm hyper aware of every part of my body, and I'm hyper aware of him sitting beside me with my leg touching his.

Thank God he looks away to the TV again before I pass out from not breathing.

His elbow's resting on the back of the couch near my head, and he's playing with his hair. I want to thread my fingers through his. I want to entwine them in his hair.

His profile's perfect. His lashes are long, his nose just the right size and shape, his lips full and kissable.

He laughs and turns to me. I flash my eyes to the screen and laugh too, even though I have no idea what we're laughing about.

He turns back to the screen, but as he does, he rests his open hand on my knee.

I'm in shock that he'd touch me again after I freaked yesterday, and I'm feeling very hot all of a sudden.

Every once in a while, his fingers bend, stroking my leg, making my breathing jagged. I hope he can't hear it.

He turns his head to look at me again. This time I don't move my eyes from his. I don't pretend I wasn't staring. He leans toward me, his lips get closer to mine, and I hold my breath. Then he stops and opens his mouth like he's going to say something, but he doesn't. Instead, he stands up. "I'm going to bed before I crash out here on your couch. See you tomorrow."

I'm still holding my breath as he turns the doorknob and leaves.

• • •

After a fitful night of trying to not think of Chris's hand on my leg, Addy and I are at the park.

With Gail and Jonathan.

We're sitting on a bench under a wispy, spindly tree. She's trying to avoid Janine for some reason and keeps looking over her shoulder toward the park entrance, watching for her.

"Do you know of anyone who babysits?" I ask. "I'll need someone to watch Addy when I get a job."

"There's a lady over on Elm Grove. I don't know her, but she has a sign in her yard sometimes when she has an opening. You could check with her. It's a little brick house with a red door. About halfway down Elm Grove on your left. You can't miss it. Her name's Terry Woods, I think."

"Thanks. I'll check it out."

I commit *Elm Grove, brick house, red door, Terry Woods* to memory by repeating it in my head ten times.

Gail peers back toward the park entrance again. She's wearing the red bandanna around her head that I thought was for gardening.

"What's the deal with Janine?" I ask, not really caring, but sitting in silence is making me crazy.

Jonathan's throwing rocks down the slide. The other kids' parents look murderous. We'll have to leave soon.

"She's such a gossip. She thrives on drama. When there isn't any, she'll make some. I just don't want to be in her cross fire." She looks over her shoulder.

I'm pushing Addy's stroller back and forth, and she lets out a little mewl when the sun shines in on her through the thin branches. Vampire baby hates the sun—that's one thing I've learned about her, other than the puking.

"Why would she gossip about you?" I stop pushing Addy's

stroller when it rests in a patch of shade, and stretch out on the bench. I need a nap after last night's flipping and flopping around instead of sleeping.

She sighs. "Long story."

I expected her to say she didn't know why, or there was no reason, not that it was a long story. It's almost like she wants me to ask her about it.

A loud cry erupts from the swings. Gail hops up and runs to Jonathan, who's lying on the ground holding his leg. He jumped. He'll kill himself one day if he doesn't stop acting like a freaking maniac.

I push Addy over to them. "Is he okay?" I shout over Jonathan's screaming.

"I don't think it's broken," Gail says.

She hoists him up and gives him a piggyback ride all the way home.

I run inside the house and grab my car keys, set on finding Terry Woods on Elm Grove so I can get Addy settled with a sitter and earn some money for us to live.

Terry's house sits on a hill. The driveway's dug in, so it's like driving into a tunnel.

I press Addy against my shoulder and make my way up the concrete steps to the house. There's a broken shutter hanging like a loose tooth from the front window. Deep claw marks are scratched into the middle of the door. I look down just in time to avoid a big pile of dog crap—it must be one huge dog.

My eyes catch the corner of a faded black and red Beware of Dog sign stuck in the overgrown tangle of weeds and bushes beside the front stoop, just as a pair of paws strike the door with a bang and a thunderous bark.

Addy jolts awake, completely defenseless and screaming

for her life, and I'm dripping with sweat and barely breathing.

The door swings open before I knock, and there's a large woman standing there screaming, "Back, Spike! Back!" She kicks one foot toward a black and tan monster of slobbering, growling, craziness. A toddler in a diaper squirms under her arm. He has matted blond hair and what looks like grape jelly smeared all over his chest.

She gives me an irritated look. "Yes?"

My eyes dart between her and Cujo, who is frantically trying to get past her leg to bite mine off. "Never mind. I have the wrong house. Sorry to bother you."

I turn and hustle down the walkway, back to the car. My hands fly with the buckles on Addy's seat belts so we can get the hell out of here before the frazzled woman releases her dog on us.

I peel out of the driveway and press my back into the seat. "That was a total nightmare, Add. There's no way I can leave you there."

I glance back in the rearview mirror at the fuzzy hair on top of Addy's head. Every now and then she lets out a screech of indignation.

"You mad at that dog for waking you up?"

She shrieks.

"Yeah. You tell him." I crack up at her baby fists waving in the air. She's going to be ferocious when she's older.

I have no idea what to do now, but I decide to drive around and see if there's a day care nearby. If I can't find one, I'll stop back home and ask Mrs. B if she knows of any place close. I don't know why I'm bothering. Day cares are way too expensive.

At the first big intersection, I turn right. No day cares so far. I pass a mall and a big fitness center. There are a couple of car dealerships, a sports bar, a hair salon, and a bike shop, but no daycares. Don't kids live in this town? Or do all the moms stay home?

I'm turning left when the idea hits me, and I make a quick U-turn.

I find a spot right up front in the Fitness Plus parking lot. A fan blows down hard on us when I push the tinted glass door open. It's a wind tunnel in the vestibule.

A girl stands behind the counter, popping her gum and talking on the phone. She's about my age, I can tell. She eyes me up and down and tells her friend to hold on.

"Can I help you?" A fake smile smears her glossed lips.

"I'd like some information, please." I switch Addy to my other shoulder.

The girl pulls out a brochure and unfolds it on the counter in front of me. "We're open seven days a week, five a.m. to nine p.m. Here's a list of classes we offer." She points to the right side of the brochure. "We have a track, racquetball courts, stationary bikes, step machines, ellipticals, treadmills, free weights, and an Olympic-size pool." She takes a deep breath, preparing for the next part of her memorized pitch. "Trainers are available by signing up here at the front desk ahead of time, and the Kids Club is staffed with certified childcare specialists."

Bingo.

"How much is a membership?" I reach for my money, inside the diaper bag, between the diapers and the bottles.

"It's usually one fifty to join and sixty a month, but right now we have a promotion going on, so your membership fee is waived and the first month is free." She snaps her gum and darts an anxious glance at the phone.

"Perfect. Do you have a form I fill out?" You're not

supposed to leave your kids there when you're not in the gym, but it's cheaper than day care, even if they do close at nine, and I'm not sure what my schedule will be when I find a job. I'll figure something out. I didn't think I'd even get this far.

I fill out the application with Addy fussing and squirming, and we head home right before she has a meltdown. It's time for her to catch some z's.

"Leah."

I roll to my back but don't open my eyes. "Hmm?"

I hear Chris's whispered laugh. "Are you hungry? We saved you some spaghetti."

My eyes snap open and focus on his, shining in the dark. I gasp and sit up. "What time is it?" I put Addy down for a nap at four and lay down on my bed for a few minutes to rest.

"Seven. You were tired."

My hands run down my face. "Oh my God! Where's Addy?" I swing my legs out of the bed, but he pushes me back onto my pillow.

"Relax. She's fine. Grandma's got her, and she's not ready to give her up yet anyway."

"But it's been hours!"

He sits on my bed. "It's no big deal." There's a curious look in his eye.

"What?" I ask.

He sucks on his bottom lip as he thinks of how to say what's on his mind. "Addy's dad. What's the deal with him?"

"What do you mean?" Shit, I don't have a story for this. My mind races.

"Why aren't you with him?"

"He's not a nice guy." That'll work.

"Why not? What did he do?"

"He . . . I don't know. I just have to stay away from him."

"Did he hit you? Is that why you ran? Did he threaten you?"

I nod, thankful that he gave me an out without me having to make up anything more.

"He can't hurt you here. You're safe." Chris pulls me into a hug. "Addy's safe here."

I inhale deeply, taking in the scent of him. I've waited for this my whole life.

My stomach growls loudly, which makes Chris laugh. "Come on."

He takes my hand and leads me down the stairs and into the kitchen. "Wait until you taste this," he says, putting a plate of spaghetti and meatballs into the microwave. He presses the buttons, licks his finger, and smiles at me.

I peer into the living room, where Mrs. B has Addy snuggled on her lap. The TV's on—some old detective show, it sounds like—there's a guy named Columbo. I know this because the volume is turned up loud. Old people can't hear.

The microwave beeps. Chris sets the plate on the table and pulls out a chair. I sit down and try not to be too self-conscious that he's staring at me, waiting for me to take a bite.

I twirl spaghetti on my fork and blow off the steam before easing it into my mouth. "Whoa," I mumble with a full mouth.

Chris plops down in the chair across from me. "Told ya."

Mrs. B's spaghetti might be the best food I've ever eaten. The sauce is spicy and tangy, and I can't eat it fast enough. I'm trying not to be a pig, but I don't remember ever eating a homemade meal that didn't involve Hope making mac and cheese and hot dogs.

Chris leaves the kitchen and comes back in holding Addy. "Grandma makes the best spaghetti. She and my grandpa used to own an Italian restaurant up in Jennings. She sold it to my aunt and uncle when Gramps died. She works at a doctor's office three days a week now doing scheduling or something, but she still goes to Mariani's on the weekends and makes their sauce."

I nod, my mouth full of meatball, and wipe my lips with a napkin. Addy's got a handful of his hair, and he's trying to pry it loose. "I could eat this every day," I say.

"Me too. Hey, Grandma says she'll watch Addy if you want to come to my show Saturday in Jacksonville." He's smiling faintly, but his blue eyes are wide, expectant. I've figured out they're blue when he's happy and more green when he's tired or thinking about something.

I swallow. "Um, that's over an hour away. I don't know if I want to be that far from her."

"She'll be fine with Grandma."

"Oh, I know she will. They bonded right away."

"So, come with me." His smile makes it almost impossible to say no. But I can't leave Addy for that long. Not yet. She's still too young.

"Next time. I'm just not comfortable leaving her yet, not with anyone."

He closes his eyes and knocks on the table with his knuckles in defeat. When he opens his eyes, he smiles again. "Okay, next time. We have a local show coming up that you're not getting out of."

"I'll be there."

Addy falls asleep in the crook of his arm, with her hand gripping his finger instead of his hair. Chris, or his grandma, already changed her into her pajamas.

"Want me to lay her down upstairs?" He stands up, careful not to wake her.

"Sure. Want to watch TV?" I stand too and take my plate to the sink.

He catches my eyes. "I'd like to spend some time with you, but I have practice tonight."

All the muscles in my body tighten at the look on his face. Tonight he would've kissed me—no question about it. "Oh. Okay."

"I'm going out with the guys after, so I'll probably be home pretty late, or I'd come up."

"No girlfriends tonight, then?" I take Addy from him.

His finger hooks my hair around my ear. "No girlfriends." He tugs a hair band off of his wrist and slips it around mine. "You really need to get some of these."

We don't move, just stand there smiling like a pair of lust-struck idiots, smiling and fumbling with our newfound attraction. The feeling wraps around us like it's a real, solid thing binding us together.

"No girlfriend," he whispers.

chapter

thirteen

Three days later, I've bought more formula and diapers, and with what they cost, my remaining money won't last long. I need a freaking job. I wonder how Hope will survive at Ohio State. I don't know how she'll have time to work, with track and school. Brian will make sure she has cash for food and stuff, but I don't know if she'll take it. She somehow managed to get to eighteen with her pride intact. I have no pride.

I have a baby to support.

I have to find a job.

I sit at the table downstairs and comb through the want ads. Mrs. B strolls in and starts getting ingredients out for her sauce. She still has her heels on that she wore to work at the doctor's office. They make her feet look like canned hams stuffed into shoes. "Looking for a job?" she asks.

"Yeah. There's not much in here, though."

I flip the page and feel her watching me. "Come over here,"

she says. "I'm going to teach you how to make sauce."

I really don't want to do this now. I want to find a job, but I push the paper aside and get up. Mrs. B hands me a garlic press and two cloves of garlic. I place one on a cutting board, pick up a knife from the counter, and smash one clove with the side of the blade. The pungent smell of garlic takes over the kitchen instantly.

"This reminds me of Giovanni's," I say. "Where I used to work. It always smelled like sauce."

"What did you do there?" Mrs. B looks at me over her shoulder.

"Made pizza. It wasn't the best—your sauce is a million times better—but I liked it. I miss working there."

She taps me on the head with a wooden spoon. "I'll tell you something, girlie. You do a good job with this sauce, and I'll get you a job at Mariani's—that's my niece and nephew's restaurant. Jim—that was my husband's name—and I used to own it. They'll hire you if I ask them to."

I can't speak. I just blink at her a few dozen times.

She laughs. "Sound good?"

"I'd get paid to make sauce and—"

"Not just sauce. You'd make pasta primavera, lasagna, fettuccini alfredo, all sorts of Italian specialties from my original Mariani family recipes."

The cardboard Leaning Tower of Pisa cut out from a Giovanni's pizza box and taped to my wall back home flashes in my mind in red and white clarity. There were times when I dreamed of having my own restaurant, times when I'd daydream about traveling to Italy and learning to cook real pizza and fancy pasta dishes. But I never let those thoughts last too long. I'd slam the door shut on the fingers of those dreams after a minute or two—they'd never happen.

But *this* is happening; she can get me a job.

The garlic press slips from my grip and clatters to the floor. "Oops." I pick it up and try to remain calm even though I'm teetering on the edge of somewhere I've never been before, and it feels faintly like security.

Mrs. B rattles off instructions, and I execute them, grabbing herbs and opening jars of tomatoes from her garden that she canned last fall. I add all the ingredients to the big pan on the stove and stir as it simmers. "It's starting to smell like yours," I say.

"Look at the smile on your face." She flicks me with a kitchen towel. "You'd think you just won the lottery."

I laugh. She has no clue that I *have* won the lottery, and not just because of the sauce.

My eyes wander around the room. It's clean. The curtains have ruffles. The cupboards are filled with food.

I have a new life.

Faith slammed the door on dreams, but Leah—Leah can have any dream she wants.

I shake my head. First, pay rent. Keep diapers on Addy. Don't get ahead of yourself, *Leah*. I kick Leah down a few pegs before she carries us both away.

Hair pulled back? Check.

Black Walmart pants I picked up at eleven o'clock last night, after Addy was asleep? Check. Thank God for Chris staying with her while I went shopping.

White T-shirt borrowed from Chris? Check. He saved me again.

Mrs. B works fast. She taught me how to make sauce a couple of days ago, and I start at Mariani's today.

At four thirty, with my big bag over my shoulder, hopefully

looking like it contains my gym clothes instead of just diapers and bottles, I head to Fitness Plus.

Bubblegum Girl waves me by as I flash my card.

"Add, you have to be a good girl." I try to catch her eye, but she's mesmerized by the fluorescent lights overhead. "I'll be back for you a little bit later." She clicks her tongue.

The woman in the Kids Club room is all smiles and high-pitched baby voices. She takes Addy from my arms with an exaggerated "Heellooo, baaabbyy!" Addy grips a clump of her dyed red hair that's the texture of straw. The woman pries Add's fingers open while making faces and cooing noises.

At least there's no vicious dog here. Kooky women I can handle.

I leave the bag of diapers and bottles and tell the lady I'm taking several classes and swimming for a while after, but I'll be back later.

Then I pry myself away, like she pried Addy's fingers from her hair, and leave.

I'm driving to work with my mind spinning in circles as fast as my mom's busted washer that never gets clothes clean, just leaves rust stains behind.

I just dumped Addy at the gym and left.

I abandoned her there.

If something happens to her, I won't be there, and they won't know where I am.

I squeeze the wheel harder so I don't give in and turn around. We need money. I can't keep her if I can't buy formula and diapers and have somewhere for us to live.

I keep telling myself this, but I still feel like crap and I'm as paranoid as my mom on bad weed. What if they call me over the loudspeaker? Shit. This isn't going to work. I should just go back and get her.

I keep arguing with myself until I'm through the door at Mariani's and introducing myself to Gretchen, Chris's cousin, who's supposed to train me.

"I'm glad you're here," she says, with red lipstick smudged on her front tooth. "I've been cooking and waiting tables by myself for the past two weeks. I'm about ready to walk out and leave my mom to do it all herself. Come in the back with me, and we'll get started."

I follow her through a swinging door into the kitchen, watching her long black ponytail swish across her back. She's probably in her midtwenties. She doesn't look much older than Chris.

There's a dishwashing area where a bunch of dirty dishes are stacked, waiting to be rinsed and run through the dishwasher. I hear someone whistling farther back in the kitchen, maybe whoever washes dishes? I hope so. I hope it's not my job.

"We'll keep you on nights, five till eleven, four or five nights a week. My mom's got the schedule for next week at home, so I'll call you tomorrow and let you know when you work next."

Gretchen leans her hands on top of a narrow countertop that looks like it's one big white cutting board. "Here's where you make salads." She lifts a stainless-steel lid on a cooler system to reveal plastic buckets of lettuce, carrots, cherry tomatoes, and salad dressing. "First put a handful of lettuce in a bowl and weigh it to make sure it's not over three and a half ounces."

I try to pay attention, but my mind is a scattered mess. It's like the big pile of dog crap on Terry Woods's walkway. I can't focus, but whatever. If I can't throw lettuce into a bowl, then I'm screwed, because this is the kind of job I'm going to have for the rest of my life. If I ever had a shot at going to college, it's gone now. I can barely manage a part-time job with Addy; there's no way I can add school into the mix.

I shouldn't even be thinking about college. I didn't even finish my junior year. How am I going to graduate high school when all I do is make bottles and change diapers?

Addy will need a bottle in a half hour. Did I tell the kids' club lady? Shit, I don't think I did.

"Leah?" Gretchen's staring at me. "Are you okay?"

"Fine. Sorry."

A slow, sympathetic smile eases over her lips. "First time you've left your baby with a sitter?" She rubs my arm. She smells like flowers.

"Yeah." I exhale fast and loud and get a head rush. Spots blink in front of my eyes, and I sway on my feet.

"Okay. Okay." Gretchen's hand clutches my wrist. "Come sit down. Have you eaten today?"

"No." I stumble behind her to a beat-up chair beside the time clock.

"Put your head between your knees before you pass out." She nudges my shoulder. I lean over and watch her feet traipse away.

The pattern on the chipped tile makes me even dizzier.

It's the stress.

The exhaustion.

Not eating.

Are all moms this pathetic, or is it just me? Because I'm a freaking disaster. Red, itchy bumps have formed on my palms, and my fingers are peeling. Every time I brush my hair, it's like I'm shedding, and my jaw aches from grinding my teeth all night.

I'm a mess. How could I have thought taking Addy was a good idea?

I didn't.

Because I didn't think about it at all.

Because it was fucking crazy.

"Here." Gretchen's shoes have pink and white striped laces. I didn't notice before.

I sit up, and she hands me a cup of Italian wedding soup and two packs of crackers. "Can this be taken out of—"

She waves me off. "Don't worry about it. It's on the house. Just eat so you don't fall over during your shift."

I take a spoonful. It's steaming hot, and so good that I lick the back of the spoon. My stomach jolts, so I tear open a pack of crackers. "Thanks, Gretchen."

"You're welcome." She brushes her hands over the front of her apron. "It gets easier. But you have to take care of yourself, or you won't do that little girl any good."

When I'm done eating, she finishes training me on the fine art of salad making, shows me where the drink station is, and teaches me how to roll silverware. Then I'm given a coffee-pot tutorial, with emphasis on keeping decaf and regular separate so as to not send anyone into cardiac arrest.

She tosses me a black apron. I have to start as a waitress, but I'll work my way up to learning the ropes in the kitchen.

My first duty is to wipe down the ancient laminated menus, which are covered with crusted splatters of red sauce. Looking under the tables, the Cheerios crushed into the carpet confirm my suspicion that I've found employment at the local kid-friendly food joint.

Addy will never grind Cheerios into the carpet under restaurant tables. Never. Not. Ever.

The soapy water stings my hands at first as I dip my rag into the bucket and start on the pile of menus. The front door opens, and two old ladies come in. They don't wait to be seated like the sign says.

What the hell?

Why believe everything you read?

"Psst!" Gretchen sticks her head out of the kitchen door. She points to the women. "Take them menus." She gives me a smile and a thumbs-up before disappearing back behind the door.

On my way to the old women's table, I'm overtaken by the image of tugging the band out of the back of Chris's hair and running my fingers through it. I lick my lips and smile at the thought.

This is how I'll get through my shift: daydreaming about being with Chris.

The old women order decaf coffee with cream, and spaghetti dinners with sweet-and-sour dressing on their salads. I never knew there was such a thing as sweet-and-sour dressing, but it's the senior-citizen standard, from what Gretchen told me.

I take the old ladies their decaf and salads and join Gretchen in the kitchen. "Two spaghetti dinners," I say, handing her the ticket.

"Already on it. Told you that's what all old people order." She smiles with her red-lipsticked lips. She has the thickest, shiniest black hair I've ever seen. Her eyes are so dark, I can't see her pupils.

I watch as she lowers a metal strainer filled with two precooked and premeasured spaghetti portions into hot water. "My aunt says you and Chris are pretty tight."

"We're good friends." I pick up a handful of pepperoni and sift it through my fingers, counting. Thirteen slices of pepperoni on a large pizza at Giovanni's. Lucky thirteen.

"I used to make him play house. He had to be the daddy, of course."

Kind of like what I'm doing now. Chris is good at playing daddy. Maybe I should thank her for training him.

"What's your baby's name?" she asks.

"Addy." My voice creaks. Was that condemnation I heard in her tone?

"How old?"

"A little over two months." I tuck my hands into my apron and ball my fists.

"It's not easy, huh?" Her eyes leave the spaghetti and turn to me. She blinks slowly and smiles. "I had my son when I was eighteen."

"Oh." My hands relax.

"I had my family around to help, though. Aunt Ivy told my mom you're from Ohio. It has to be insanely hard for you." She pulls the strainer out of the water and divvies the pasta into two bowls.

"Chris and Mrs. B have been a lot of help. I'm lucky I found them." I wish I had Hope. She loves babies. Brian's older sister has a one-year-old little girl. Once when I was over at Brian's with Hope, the baby was there and Hope sat on the floor playing with her the entire time. Hope would love Addy—assuming she could get past the part where I kidnapped Addy and took off.

"Chris is a good guy," Gretchen says.

There's a hint of a threat in her eyes.

Why does everyone assume I'll hurt him?

They must be clairvoyant.

After the old women eat and leave, I get only two more tables before it's 8:40. I've made enough in tips to buy precisely three-fourths of a can of formula.

I'm so screwed, and I have to fake my way out of here to pick up Addy.

I clutch my stomach and find Gretchen in the back making a pizza for a to-go order. "Hey, I'm not feeling very well," I tell her. "You know how I almost passed out earlier? I think I might be getting the flu or something. I need to leave."

Her eyebrows shoot up. "You want to leave? Why don't you just sit down for a while? You only have a couple more hours."

Shit.

I drop down in the chair by the time clock again and fold my arms over my stomach. The clicking of the clock over my head is making me crazy. I have to get out of here and pick up Addy. "I'm going to puke." I bolt through the kitchen door and jog across the dining room, into the ladies' room.

I catch my reflection in the mirror and hate what I see.

A liar.

A kidnapper.

A high school dropout.

God, I can't believe I did this to myself.

Then Addy creeps into my mind, followed by an image of my mom in her ratty robe, and I don't regret any of it. Living with Angel and Dave would be even worse with the constant partiers hanging out all night and drugs everywhere. I got us out of there. We won't live like that no matter how many lies I have to tell. We'll have a better life than that . . . *somehow.*

I hold my breath until my face turns red, then splash some water on it to make it look clammy. Gretchen's waiting on a table when I come out of the bathroom. "I have to go," I tell her when she's on her way back to the kitchen. "I just threw up," I whisper, so the customers don't hear.

"Okay," she says. I can tell she's pissed. Why would she be pissed if I puked and have to leave? She must not believe me.

I can't worry about that now.

I head to my car and fly down the road toward Fitness Plus, darting glances in the rearview mirror every few seconds.

The last thing I need is a speeding ticket in a stolen car.

When I get to the Kids Club and open the door, there's a different woman watching the kids. Addy's screaming in a crib, and another little boy is sitting on the floor throwing blocks at the wall.

The new lady glares at me. "We didn't have enough bottles. We paged you five times."

My stomach drops to the floor.

My heart pounds in my head.

I can't swallow.

"I'm—"

"We've had moms like you before." She glances at my chest, making me all too aware of the nametag still pinned there. "This isn't a daycare; it's to be utilized by parents who are here, on the premises to work out. You're lucky you're here. I was just about to call the police." She gestures to the clock. It's five after nine.

I have no idea what to say. What *can* I say? "I'm sorry. I didn't—"

"You didn't have anyone else to watch her." She takes a step toward me and crosses her arms over her chest. "Maybe you should've thought about that before deciding to raise a baby. There's always adoption, you know."

I feel my face contort with rage. "Fuck off."

I grab Addy and her bag while the lady tells me my membership card is no longer valid. At least I got one night of free babysitting out of the deal.

The girl behind the counter snaps her gum and smirks when she sees me. She's flipping through a magazine. I slam my hand down on top of it. "And fuck you, too."

chapter

fourteen

Chris is fiddling with an old guitar he's fixing up for this guy, Manny, who owns the bar in Jacksonville where his band plays. "It's a fifty-nine Gibson Les Paul Flame Top," he says, wrapping a guitar string around his finger.

His drummer, Aaron, stopped by to drop off the guitar. He glances at me for my reaction.

"Yeah, I have no idea what that means." Addy squawks beside me. I shift the patio chair where I have her lying, nestled in a blanket, out of the sun. It's got to be ninety degrees out. I would love nothing better than to jump in the pool, but I don't have a bathing suit.

"It means that guitar is worth more than Chris's truck," Aaron says. He laughs and taps a rhythm on the glass table-top with his index fingers.

Chris laughs too. "It also means that I can charge him an assload to fix it." He turns a little silver knob that tightens the string. "Not many people know how to repair vintage guitars like this—at least not well."

"How'd you learn?" I ask, leaning forward to watch him work.

"Gramps." He tugs on his cap, like a tribute to his grandpa.

"Shit, man," Aaron says, "you need to ditch that roofing job and do this full-time. You saw that Les Paul sell on eBay the other night for ninety-eight grand. Dude, you're missing your calling."

Chris just shrugs. "Yeah."

I can't decide if I like Aaron. He's either the best guy ever, since he's Chris's friend, or the complete ass he's coming off as to me. Considering the difference in definition alone, I shouldn't have such a huge problem putting my finger on it, but he's a hard one to peg. Plus, I've only known him for a half hour. But he has this swagger and cocky smile that make me want to punch him in the face.

"You work tonight?" Chris asks, glancing up at me through his thick eyelashes.

"No." I dart a glance at Aaron and watch him take a deep drag on his cigarette. "I'm not sure when I work next. I need to check with Gretchen."

When Chris found out Mrs. B got me a job, he'd asked where I was leaving Addy while I worked. I'd told him I got a sitter for her and changed the topic. I don't need him to know I'm the world's worst person ever for abandoning her at Fitness Plus last night. He'd probably hate me forever. He likes Addy better than me anyway—or at least as much.

I called Gretchen earlier today and told her my childcare fell through. She asked how I was feeling, and I could tell she still wasn't convinced that I'm sick. I was waiting for her to release me to my destiny by giving me the it's-not-working-out speech, but she didn't. Yet. She told me to let her know when I could be put back on the schedule.

"Speaking of Gretchen," Mrs. B says, banging through the screen door, "she just called me. Why didn't you tell me you needed a sitter for Addy? I would've waited until you had childcare before I told her you could start working."

Great, I let Mrs. B down. She gets me a job and I bail the first night. I'm such a loser. I wouldn't blame her if she hates me now. "Sorry. I thought I had it worked out, but I had to pick up Addy by nine."

"So you told Gretchen you were sick." She purses her lips and fiddles with the top button on her shirt.

I nod, glancing at Chris. He's smirking. He thinks this is funny. Jerk.

Aaron's still drumming his fingers like he's oblivious.

"Well . . . ," Mrs. B says, her face melting a little from its sour expression. "Just be honest with us from now on. I can watch the little one if—"

"No." I can't let her down again. There's no way I'm accepting more help. "Thanks, but you've done a lot for me already. I don't want to take advantage—"

"Don't ever think you're taking advantage of me!" She smacks my arm. "You live here. You're like a part of the family now. You have no idea how much I've missed my Kay—" She clamps her mouth shut and glances down at her feet. "How much I've missed having a baby around."

I can practically feel Chris's entire body tense. It reverberates through the air.

Mrs. B takes a deep breath and smiles. "I thought I heard Aaron out here." She leans down and squeezes his shoulders. "How are you, dear? Can I get you three something to drink? It's a hot one today." She fans the neck of her shirt in and out.

"You should go for a swim, Mrs. B." Aaron taps his fingers on the table again. I wonder if he drums on the pillows when he sleeps.

"Heavens no! I'm too old to put on a swimsuit." She pats her hair into place. "Why don't you let me watch the little one for a while so you young kids can go have some fun?"

Chris lays the guitar on the table, scoots his chair back, and stretches. "I'm getting hungry. You guys want to get something to eat?"

"I gotta get going," Aaron says, stubbing out his cigarette on the thick sole of his Doc Marten boot. "Told Manny I'd fill in for him behind the bar tonight." He stands up and swings his arms back and forth a few times. "You two should stop in."

"It's an hour and a half away," Chris says, adjusting the tension on the guitar strings. "Kind of far to stop in."

"What else do you have to do?" Aaron says, knocking me on the shoulder with his fist like we're pals. "Hang out with this chick?" He winks at me.

I want to hit him with my fist too, but much harder . . . and not on his shoulder. There's just something about him that makes me cringe.

"Chris, take Leah and get something to eat," Mrs. B says. "Come on." She tugs his arm. "Get out of here. I want that baby to myself."

In line at the Taco Bell drive-thru, Chris glances over at me with a shit-eating grin on his face. "Gretchen busted you with Grandma."

"Shut up." I turn my head and look out the window.

He pretends to cough. "I'm so sick. I have to go home." His laugh bounces off the windows and fills the cab of the truck. "Faker."

I whip around and shove his shoulder but can't help laughing too. "Shut up!"

The line moves, and he pulls up to the speaker. "What do you want?" he asks.

"Two soft tacos and a Coke." I dig in my pocket for a couple of bucks while he orders. "Here." I hold out three dollars, and he looks at it like I'm trying to hand him one of Addy's dirty diapers.

He waves my hand away. "I'm paying."

The bills feel soggy in my sweaty hand. I stuff them back into my pocket. "Thanks."

"Why didn't you ask me to pick up Addy instead of leaving work early? I would've helped you out, you know." He rolls his window down, exchanges cash for the bag of food, and hands it over to me to hold.

I didn't ever think of asking Chris to help me. He would've, I know that, but it never crossed my mind. The thought of him coming to my rescue makes me uncomfortable. Relying on other people hasn't worked out for me in the past—well, ever. "I have to figure this out on my own—how to be a mom, I mean."

He nods. "I can respect that. But just know I'll help when you ask."

"Okay." I tie the handles of the plastic Taco Bell bag, then untie them.

"We can eat at the park. There's a lake and picnic tables. It'll be fun." He adds a smile to prove how fun it will be.

"Yeah. I've been there a couple of times with Addy and Gail and Jonathan."

A line forms between his brows. He readjusts his backward cap.

"I thought you only wear your grandpa's cap when you

play." I twist the plastic bag handles around my hand.

He shrugs. The line's still there in his forehead. "Felt like wearing it."

"Is something wrong?" I twist the handles again.

He darts a look at me, then looks back at the road. "No. It's cool."

We drive the last few blocks in silence, listening to his tool-box for his roofing job rattle around in the bed of the truck, until he pulls into a parking spot at the park. "Here, I'll carry that." Chris takes the bag off my lap, but I have to pry my fingers out of the knotted handles. My fingers are red with white stripes where the plastic dug in.

He comes around to open my door, but I've already hopped out. "Oh. Sorry. I didn't realize . . ."

"It's cool."

It's so not cool. There is something wrong with him. I said or did something I shouldn't have, or maybe I didn't say or do something I should've. I don't know. I'm a freaking idiot though, that's a given.

I follow him toward a picnic table. Three geese come out of nowhere and start nudging my legs with their beaks.

"Hey! Stop!" Chris shouts in front of me. He's surrounded by a swarm of geese poking and nipping at him. The Taco Bell bag is raised over his head.

About fifty more geese are waddling toward us at top speed. "Uh, Chris?" He looks back, and I nod toward the gaggle of approaching birds.

"Let's eat in the truck." He grabs my hand, and we run back to his truck with nipping beaks and disgruntled honks right behind us.

We both jump in and slam the doors, panting and laughing. "Look at them," he says. "They're circling."

"I think they're plotting our demise."

"I think you're right. Who knew geese ate tacos?" He puts the bag down between us and sets his drink in the cup holder. "First time I take you out, and you almost get mauled by a pack of geese with a taste for Mexican food. Perfect." He rolls his eyes and tugs on the bill of his backward cap. A hint of a smile flashes on his face.

"That would be the worst first date ever," I say, and clamp my teeth together. I can't believe I just said this was our first date. He never said this was a date. Oh. My. God. I hate myself.

His hand digs into the food bag. "Come on, the worst ever? Death by goose? I've had much worse first dates than that. Suffering through them was worse than death." He hands me my soft tacos.

I jab my straw against my leg until the end pokes out of the wrapper and I can grab it with my teeth to pull it out of the paper. "So, not many people can fix up old guitars like you?"

He shrugs and plays it off like it's no big deal. "I don't know. I know I'm good at it from the amount I get away with charging."

"Could you do it all the time, like Aaron said, instead of roofing? Would you, I mean?"

His eyes tell me he's hesitant to talk about things like this—dreams, goals, the future. I know how he feels, I just don't know why Chris would be feeling it. He has such a good life. Why would thinking about the future scare him?

"I'd love to," he says. "Dad wants me to go back to college. Get a real job." He folds the taco's wrapper down over the end of it. "I'm not really the academic type, if you haven't noticed. I'd rather get out and do things than learn about doing things."

"I can't see you sitting behind a desk in a tie," I admit.

He groans and rolls his eyes. "That would kill me. Want any sauce?" He tears open a packet of mild with his teeth while holding his taco in the other hand.

"No, thanks." I open my taco wrapper and start scraping the lettuce off, trying not to get it all over me or his seat. I hate lettuce. And tomato. All vegetables, really. We never had vegetables at my house, unless you count French fries . . . and ketchup.

"Why didn't you tell me to order it without lettuce?" The corner of Chris's mouth quirks up as he chews.

"I just pick it off." I shrug and pluck a shred of orange cheese off the seat beside me, and his hand swipes down and brushes the rest of the cheese and lettuce I've dropped onto the floor.

"You've seen my room, right? I'm not all that concerned with cheese on my seat."

"It's cool?" I tease. He always says it's cool.

He snorts and laughs, coughs a few times and swallows, then takes a long sip from his straw. "You almost made me choke. That would *not* be cool. Death by choking due to a lame attempt at mockery—worst first date ever."

"Would that make me the superhero of bad first dates?" I take a bite while he wads up his empty wrapper.

He tosses the wrapper onto the floor and tugs my hair. "Stop making fun of me, or I'll be forced to bring up your Tae Kwon Do moves on the Pack 'n Play."

Now it's my turn to laugh while I chew and try not to choke.

"Seriously, what was the deal with that? It looked like you were about to make a break for it."

I take a drink and stall while he unwraps another taco

and squirts hot sauce on top of it. "There's no deal to tell you about. It's cool."

He blinks and nods, his face falling into a stoic expression. "I see. It's cool."

He finishes his taco.

I finish mine.

We don't talk.

"Are you sure nothing's wrong?" I ask, because it's obvious that I've done it again—whatever it is that I'm doing, or not doing.

He shrinks down and leans back against his seat, making his cap lift in the front. "Nothing's wrong, Leah. I shouldn't expect you to be straight with me—we just met."

He's upset because I won't tell him what was really going on when I was kicking the Pack 'n Play—acting like I've hurt his feelings or something. "Being a martyr doesn't work with me. If you're pissed, be pissed." I shove the door open and jump out. "I didn't leave my mom to deal with someone else's shit." I slam the door and realize what I said. Shit. At least I didn't say I'm a kidnapper.

I take five steps through the gravel parking lot, and Chris grabs my arm. "Wait." I try to pull my arm free, but he won't let go. "Please, Leah, I'm sorry."

He steps in front of me. His eyes are green. Blazing green in the bright sun. He's not very happy right now. "I'm trying to get to know you." His hand drops to his side. "There's something about you that's so raw and open, but at the same time, you're the most guarded person I've ever met." He laces his fingers and rests them on top of his cap, shaking his head. "I don't know. I blew it. Come on, I'll take you back home."

He turns, and I touch his back. "There are things I can't tell anyone about. Not just you."

He glances back over his shoulder. "Did you run away? You said you left your mom."

I'm suddenly bloodless and cold. He knows. "I'm eighteen, so it's not technically running away." What's another lie? I'm already leading the parade to hell, so I might as well say I'm eighteen. "She can't find me. I won't talk about it." I look down and watch my foot scuff through the gravel.

It's the deal breaker.

I have secrets.

I can't tell him the truth, and he knows it.

His hands fall on my shoulders. "It's cool, Leah." My eyes rise to his. He's smiling. I'm not cold anymore. "I don't have any right to ask for your secrets. We just met. Maybe some-day . . ." He shrugs. "Get back in the truck before the geese realize their prey came back outside. I won't be the superhero of worst first dates ever."

"You're leaving that title to me, huh?" We start walking back to the truck. His arm's tucked around my waist.

"Not by a long shot." His finger pokes my side.

I glance at his face. He's smiling and totally oblivious of what I truly am—the superhero of guilt and deception.

Later that night, Letterman is on upstairs. Both of my legs are across Chris's lap. I'm lying on my back. His hands run up and down my bare thighs, making chords and strumming like I'm a guitar.

He still hasn't kissed me.

I might explode.

He laughs at something on TV.

I don't.

I'm annoyed.

"Didn't you think that was funny?" he asks.

"I'm not really watching." I can feel my forehead tighten.

"Why not? What's wrong?"

"What the hell is wrong with you?" I snap.

He lifts his hands off me. "Sorry."

"You're an idiot." I sit up, shaking my head.

"I'm an *idiot*?"

"How is it that you can touch me like that and not kiss me? Are you trying to make me crazy?"

He laughs. "I thought it might be too soon."

I turn my face to his and squint in confusion. "But not too soon to rub my thighs?"

"You're right. I'm an idiot."

I wait for it. "Well?"

He throws both hands in the air. "I'm not going to do it now. You're all pissed at me for not doing it."

I shove him and try not to laugh but can't help it.

"Will you stop touching me?" He laughs and scoots to the opposite end of the couch. "You're getting me all worked up."

I toss a throw pillow at his head, too embarrassed to speak.

He wings it back, and it whacks me in the face. His laugh is loud and sharp, like a bark.

"That was *not* funny!" I stand up and hurl the pillow at him again. It spins fast, corner over corner, like a Chinese star. He reaches out to grab it but misses, and it catches him between his legs.

"*Oopfh!*" he groans through a rush of air. His legs squeeze together, and he makes the time-out sign with his hands.

I suck my lips in so I don't laugh. My cheeks are so tight, they ache. "Sorry," I mutter. "I'm disqualified. You win."

Addy screams from my bedroom.

"Game over," Chris says between deep breaths. "Thank God. You're killing me."

"Next time kiss me, or wear a cup." I pad into my room feeling my cheeks turn red.

When I bring Addy out, he has a bottle ready and reaches for her. "I'll take her."

"You don't have to." Her eyes blink back and forth between the two of us a few times but then stay on him. I swear, if she could choose between us, it would be him every single time.

He sits on the couch, feeds her, and watches Letterman. I sit beside them, not sure if I'm thankful for Addy's interruption or bummed out by it.

It was fast—our attraction—and strong. If this starts . . . I'm afraid to think about it. Jason was wrong. I'm not sexually repressed after all.

chapter

fifteen

The next day, Addy and I have another walk to the park hijacked by Gail and supermaniac Jonathan. I swear I have to find an alternate route to avoid going past her house.

Janine and Emma are here too. The kids are playing in the backyard, swinging on the swing set. I sit down at the picnic table beside Janine. The sun's blazing hot. I have to hold my hand over my eyes to see Gail across the table.

Addy starts squawking and rubbing her fists over her eyes.

"Why don't you lay her under the tree, in the shade?" Gail suggests, pointing to a big, shady oak between the picnic table and the barrage of play equipment—swing set, sandbox, battery-powered Jeep—that makes her backyard look like Toys "R" Us exploded all over it.

I eye Emma and Jonathan, weighing the odds of the two of them loading Addy into the Jeep without me noticing. "All right."

As I'm spreading out Addy's blanket and getting her settled,

Gail goes inside for lemonade. This is the perfect time to talk to Janine about watching Addy. Not that I want her to, but I'm desperate, and there's no way I'm asking Gail to watch Addy with Jonathan in the same house.

I slip back onto the bench beside her and shade my eyes.

"She's a good baby," Janine says, gazing over at Addy.

Perfect opening. Maybe this was meant to be. "She really is. She hardly ever cries and takes lot of naps still during the day."

"I wanted another baby, but my husband is out of town a lot. He didn't want another kid he couldn't spend time with." She shrugs, tears her eyes from Addy, and sighs.

Crap, it seems so insensitive to ask her right now. I can't wait, though. I have to go back to Mariani's and make money. "Janine, I was wondering if you would watch Addy three or four nights a week while I'm at work. I'd pay you, of course." I have no clue how I'm going to pay her.

She taps her lip, considering. "I've always thought Emma needed another little kid around. She gets so bored watching TV and playing by herself. She has Jonathan. . . ." Janine rolls her eyes. "Those two are like a tornado together. Not that Addy could play with her, but it might be good for Emma. Kind of like a baby sister." Her head starts nodding, like it's made the decision for her without filling her in. Then her eyes find mine and light up. She smiles. "Okay. I think that would work out. What days will you bring her over, and what time?"

"I'll call and get my schedule as soon as I get home. I work from five until eleven."

Her lips pull back. "*Sheesh*, that's late."

My heart jumps. This is when she tells me no.

Then she waves it off. "It's okay, though. I'll put her to sleep at her normal time. It won't be a problem."

"You're sure?"

She puts a hand on my shoulder. "Positive." Her eyes dart behind me. "Don't even think about it!"

I turn around in time to see Jonathan give Addy a leaf covered in sand that he unburied in his sandbox. The kid's a walking hazard to Addy's short life. "No!" I lunge the ten feet from the picnic table to Addy's blanket.

He shoves her hand into her face, smashing the leaf to her lips, giggles like a lunatic, and dashes away. Addy screams, and I see sand speckling her tongue. "Asshole kid," I mutter under my breath.

I swipe my finger through her mouth, trying to collect all the grit. She's red and flailing around like I'm choking her.

"What happened?" Gail asks, charging toward me with a glass of lemonade in each hand. "What did Jonathan do now?"

"Nothing. Just playing a game. He didn't know Addy wasn't old enough to eat sand and leaves."

"Eat sand and . . . Jonathan!" She storms off after Son of Satan.

"I'm taking her home!" I yell after her, over Addy's garbled, spit-and-sand-filled shrieks.

I wave to Janine, hold Addy against me, and pull the stroller down the sidewalk behind us. "Don't worry, Add, when you're older you can get him back. You've got plenty of time to plot your revenge."

Mrs. B's head pops out the front door. "What happened to our baby?" She starts down the front steps.

"Sand in her mouth. She's okay."

Chris and his dad come out of the garage and stand in the driveway. "It's cool?" Chris asks.

"It's cool." I smile at our first inside joke.

Chris laughs and turns back toward the garage, where his dad's already disappeared again. Mrs. B tugs Addy out of my arms. "I'll get her cleaned up and settled." She presses her cheek against Addy's and mutters baby talk in her tiny ear. "Go get Chris and make him take a break. Those two have been cleaning out that garage all day. I have warm cookies inside, just out of the oven."

I cross in a diagonal path through the yard to the driveway. Chris has his back to me. The muscles in his back shift as he lifts a toolbox and sets it on a shelf. His jeans fit exactly how they should. Not tight, just snug enough in all the right places. I can't believe he didn't kiss me last night. Maybe I should just kiss him and get it over with since he keeps bailing on the idea.

Mr. Buckridge coughs. My eyes fly to where he's standing and watching me ogle his son. "Chris . . . ," he says.

Chris turns around as I die inside and vow to never be within one hundred yards of his dad again, who now has no doubt in his mind that I'm a big slutty teenage mom who wants to screw his son. Only the last part is accurate, but I don't want him to know that.

"Hey," Chris says, wiping his hands on his dirty jeans.

"Hey. Your grandma says you should take a break. She made cookies."

He wipes his sweaty forehead on his shoulder. "What time is it?"

"Around four, I think." I hook my thumbs in my pockets and rock up on my toes, darting glances at Mr. Buckridge out of the corner of my eye.

Chris steps forward and leans in to whisper in my ear. "He doesn't bite."

I push his shoulder and roll my eyes. "Are you coming in, Mr. Buckridge? Or I could bring some out if you want." I raise my brows at Chris.

"Thank you, Leah. I'll be there in just a minute. I want to

finish sorting these nails, screws, and whatever this is." He holds up an L-shaped silver rod the length of a nail and studies it.

Chris chuckles to himself and hooks my arm with his, dragging me out of the garage. "I have practice in an hour. It's my bass player, Jeremy's, birthday. The guys are bringing their girlfriends, and we're hanging out after we play."

Shit. I was hoping we could watch TV, but not really watch it this time. Guess that's out. "Well, have fun. I'll let you know what you miss on Letterman." I grab the handle on the back door, but he pulls me out back to the patio.

"I think you missed the part where you're coming with me." He tugs my hair. His eyes are the same color as the pool water.

"I think you missed the part where you ask me." I'm trying to ignore the pricks of sweat bursting out all over my body.

"I said the guys . . ." He sighs and runs his hands over his face and up through his hair. "Would you go with me? I'd like you to."

I think he's implying I'm his girlfriend.

I can't swallow.

He hasn't even kissed me yet.

I can actually see my heart pounding when I glance down at my chest.

"What about Addy? I'd have to bring her."

"Addy can stay with me!" Mrs. B calls through the screen door. I swear she has ears like a bat except when Columbo's on TV. "Not that I was listening to you two."

"Thanks, Gram," Chris answers. Then he holds my eyes for a few seconds, which feels like forever. "Well?"

"Yeah. Sure, okay. I'll go with you." My insides are freaking out. I'm going to either puke or scream. Maybe both.

This can't be happening. I came here to escape a life, not make a new one. Everything's too screwed up to start something this good. It's like putting whipped cream on moldy leftovers.

He doesn't even know my real name.

He thinks I'm eighteen.

He's going to end up hating me. I don't think I can take that.

"You know what? Maybe I should stay with Addy." I glance over my shoulder to the screen door. I can't see inside, but I can hear the clinks and clatters of pots and pans and dishes.

His touch on my arm makes my head jerk back around. "Come with me. It'll be fun." He tucks my hair behind my ear. "Anyway, I'm the superhero of best second dates. You wouldn't want to miss that."

God, I so wouldn't. Especially if it involves his wide, perfect lips on mine. "Okay. I'll go change."

His eyes run over me. "You look fine." He gestures to his jeans and T-shirt—which doesn't have a superhero on it today. "I'm wearing this. We're just hanging out in Jeremy's basement. No big deal."

I wonder what the other girls will be wearing. Somehow I don't think my ratty cutoff khakis will impress anyone. "You look good. I'm a mess." Then I realize if his friends already know that I'm a runaway teen with a baby, they think I'm a trash ball anyway. I don't know why I'm going to bother.

"I'm sweaty and dirty. I've been cleaning out the garage all day, and you think I look good?" He grins. "I like you more and more all the time."

My ears and neck are burning. "I'll be right back. I need to call Gretchen anyway and tell her I can be scheduled to work again. Janine from down the street is going to watch Addy."

"Oh, the gossip hound. Perfect. Can't wait to hear all about the scandalous things we're doing together when the rumors get back to my grandma."

He laughs, and my face burns even more thinking about

us being scandalous together. "Be right back." I dart inside. Mrs. B and Addy aren't in the kitchen, but I catch a glimpse of them through the front door, sitting on the porch. My feet take the stairs two at a time, and I lean against my door after closing it.

He said he likes me more and more all the time. I have to go for it or push him away. Even considering pushing him away is a lie. I can't do it. I'm already too completely gone over him. That leaves me with one option—go for it. Tonight.

Chris sits on a wobbly stool with his black Converse high-tops resting on the wooden rails between its legs. I love the way his fingers work, back and forth, light then hard, gripping and thrumming his guitar strings.

His grandpa's cap is pulled on backward, and his eyes are closed as he belts out the last notes of the ballad he's singing. His voice gives me goose bumps. It sounds so different from when he talks and laughs.

It's hot in jeans, sitting on a rump-sprung chair in Jeremy's basement. Jeremy's and Aaron's girlfriends are huddled together on a beat-up couch, talking about the high-heeled sandals one of them just bought.

Who the hell cares? I'm so beyond worrying about the latest shoes. I'm pretty much at the worrying-if-you-*have*-shoes part of life. I tried to be nice to them and join their conversation, but I have nothing to add to a discussion about lip gloss and hair highlights.

They ignore me. It works for all of us. I just want to listen to Chris sing and wish they'd shut the hell up.

He ends the song, and the band talks about a part they want to change. The girls are still jabbering. I don't think they realize the music stopped—or they don't care. I feel stupid sitting here, like I wandered in off the street.

I shouldn't be here.

I should be with Addy.

I have to go home.

I stand up and move toward the basement door, catching Chris's eye. "Leah?" He saunters over to me. "Where are you going?"

My hand fumbles with the doorknob. "I should go. It's not far. I can walk."

His eyes pop open wide. "Did something happen?" He shoots a glance at the girls on the couch. "Are they ignoring you? I'll say something to them."

I grip his arm tight. "No! Don't say anything. It's not their fault. I just don't have much in common with them."

He snorts. "No, you don't. Thank God. Those girls would drive me crazy." He looks back over at them. "There's no substance—not to either of them. All fluff." He shakes his head and rests his hands on my hips. "You get it. You know life's about more than the mall." He lifts his chin, nodding back behind him to his band. "And I know we're never going to be rock stars. Those guys don't."

I want to get out of here and just be alone with him—anywhere—doing anything.

"Come on." He sits down on the couch and pulls me onto his lap. All eyes are on us now.

"Chris—catch." Jeremy tosses him a can of beer from the basement fridge. "Want one, Leah?" Jeremy seems like a cool guy. He has shaggy black hair and a big nose and laughs a lot in a raspy voice.

"Umm . . . no, thanks."

"Here, babe." Jeremy hands a can to his girlfriend, Angie,

with a kiss. She's tiny, with blond hair and a voice like a second grader, all cute and high pitched.

Jeremy takes Angie's feet onto his lap and slips her shoes off.

I shift on Chris's lap, not used to how it feels and wishing it had happened in private before happening in public. He's an idiot.

Aaron plops down in the chair I'd been sitting in. "What's up, Leah? What'd you think of that last song? Chris wants to open the show with it, but I think it's too slow. We need something bigger"—he smacks his hands together—"louder, don't you think?"

Chris's hand finds chords up and down my back. Before I can answer, Aaron's girlfriend—the one with the new sandals—moves to sit on the floor at Aaron's feet and chimes in. "You totally need something explosive to start a show. You don't want to lose them during the first song." She admires her new shoes and runs her fingers through her freshly highlighted hair.

"I didn't ask you, Vee," Aaron says, taking her can and opening it for her.

"You never have to ask." She smacks his leg. "My opinions are given freely."

Maybe she's okay after all.

"Well?" Chris asks, pushing my hair aside so he can see my face. "What do you think?"

I have zero experience with song selections for shows. I don't really know. "Whatever you guys think. . . ."

"I think we need to try this weed I got from Manny." Aaron pulls a baggie out of his pocket. "Got my pipe?" he asks Vee.

She opens her purse and pulls out a pipe. "Here."

Jeremy pushes Angie's legs off of his lap, gets up, and fishes his own pipe out of his guitar case. "Manny got some great shit from some Cuban supplier," he tells Chris.

Chris doesn't say anything, just nods.

"It better be good," Angie says. "You've been talking about it for a week, making me crazy." She laughs and takes a drink of her beer.

I'm stiff and rigid.

"What's wrong?" Chris whispers in my ear.

"Nothing." I don't look at him.

Aaron and Jeremy fill and light their pipes. The familiar smell of sweet smoke fills the room. The image of me flushing Mom's down the toilet comes to mind.

Vee crawls onto Aaron's lap and kisses him. He blows smoke into her mouth. Beside us, Angie pulls her shirt over her head, revealing a low-cut tank top underneath, and straddles Jeremy's lap. He passes her the pipe, and she takes a deep drag and holds it in.

With the stripping, kissing, and smoking, I'm ready to bolt.

I stand. "I'm going home."

Chris yanks me back down on the couch. "What? Why?" he whispers.

I look around. "I'm not into this." I pull my hand free.

His finger hooks my belt loop. "Fine. I'll take you home."

I don't wait for him to tell his friends good-bye, just walk directly toward the stairs. I hear mutterings about us going to be alone and how he's lucky he lives with his chick and can get busy anytime.

I hustle up the steps and wait for him outside in his truck.

He comes out looking super pissed. If I could see his eyes in the dark, they'd be green for sure. He gets in and slams his door. "What's wrong with you?"

"You're the superhero of worst second dates ever—that sucked!" I lean my forehead against the passenger-side window and stare out. It hits me that he shouldn't be driving. I turn to him and hold out my hand. "Give me your keys."

"I'm fine." He starts the engine.

I open my door and hop out. "Fine. I'll walk."

"Jesus Christ, Leah." He scoots over to the passenger side. "Happy?"

I drive us home. We don't speak. He blasts the radio.

We get out of the truck, and he storms to the back patio, following me. "What did I do?"

I hate arguing. I've argued with my mom all my life, and I'm exhausted with it. "Nothing."

He squeezes my shoulders. "Don't tell me 'nothing.' I did something to make you want to leave. Tell me what I did."

My mind flashes back to the party, the beer, the weed. "It's me, not—"

"Don't give me that it's-me-not-you bullshit, Leah. Tell me what's up your ass."

"What's up my ass?" I put my hands on his shoulders and try to shove him away. He doesn't budge. "What's up my ass?" I shove again, getting more pissed every second. "I didn't take Addy and leave my drugged-out whore mom to have it shoved down my throat again, asshole! That's what's up my ass!" I bring my knee up, and he hunches over to protect himself. I shove his shoulders, and he crashes backward into the pool.

He surfaces, coughing and sputtering, wiping his face and dumping water out of his grandpa's cap. He staggers up the pool stairs and stalks toward me. "I didn't know. You can't be pissed at me for putting you in that situation. You don't tell me anything about yourself. How was I supposed to know?"

He keeps coming closer. I step back. "It doesn't matter if you didn't know. It's the fact that you were there."

He takes two more steps forward. I take two more back and

hit the side of the garage. "Did you see me smoke pot? No. That's my band. I have to be there. You don't have to go again. I won't ask. I'm sorry it sucked."

Two more steps—we're touching. Water from his clothes is dripping onto me. His hands press against the garage on both sides of my head. His eyes drill into mine. "I want to know you. If I know you, I won't piss you off."

We're both breathing hard. That's all I hear. It blocks the buzz of the outside light and the chirp of crickets. I feel my head nod, but I didn't move it. My hands hold his forearms, but I don't remember putting them there.

Chris's face eases closer, and there's a roar in my ears—my blood rushing hard and fast. His eyes fall to my lips. It's all slow motion—his lips barely touch mine, feather light, breath mingling, lips closing on mine, opening, deepening. He leans in to me, pressing our bodies together. His hand finds the side of my face. His thumb traces my brow. His other arm wraps around my waist and holds me against him—secure.

My head swims. If it weren't for him holding me down, I'd float away. I squeeze him tight, memorizing the feel of his back beneath my hands. Our kisses turn urgent, hungry, and desperate. His hand moves over me, and I break away, throwing my head back for more air before I pass out. His lips trail down my neck.

Inside, Addy cries. I push his shoulders, and he lifts his head. Our lips meet a few more times as the dizzy, heady feeling subsides.

"I have to go in."

He leans his forehead against mine as he nods. "I know. I'll come with you."

I grin. "I figured you would. You live here."

He steps back and takes my hands. "There you go making fun of me again."

"It's just too easy sometimes." I poke his side, and he twists. "Don't."

"Ticklish?" I poke him again.

He chuckles and pulls me toward the house. "Me? Ticklish? Never."

"Good. The superhero of the best second date ever shouldn't be ticklish. It's not cool."

"Shut up," he teases, and drapes his arm around my neck. "Get inside and take care of your kid, would ya?" He nudges me with his hip. "I'll get the bottle ready."

At the screen door, I stop him and kiss him again, soft this time. "Thank you."

"For what?"

"Everything."

The next two nights, Chris and I watch Letterman between making out on my couch and Addy waking up for a bottle. The day after, I'm back at Mariani's. Janine was all smiles when I dropped Addy off. She told me not to worry, she'd keep her away from Jonathan. It seems to be common knowledge that a pack of wolves causes less destruction than that kid.

Four tables come and go, leaving me with almost eight dollars. The food's cheap, and so are the customers. I'm praying for at least another four tables by the end of the night, but Mondays are incredibly slow.

"Leah," Gretchen calls from the kitchen, "come back here and help me make this to-go order."

I dash to the back, hoping tonight is the night I get to cook something. I'm not really cut out to be a waitress. The general public tends to annoy me, especially all the cheap old people who leave fifty-cent tips.

Gretchen's cooking apron makes me want to crack up. She's so tall and thin, it looks like a giant brown sack looped around her neck that just hangs off of her. "You can make the deluxe alfredo pizza." She pulls a large pan out of the cooler with a lump of cold dough on it and slides it down the pizza bar toward me.

"Okay." I shove up my sleeves, pry the cold dough off the pan, and spread some oil over it so the crust doesn't stick.

"The alfredo sauce is in the cooler underneath." She taps a stainless-steel door at my knees. "You'll find the precooked chicken breasts in there too. I'll be making salads. Yell if you need me."

I've already learned what goes on the alfredo pizza—alfredo sauce, cheese, grilled chicken, and mushrooms. The deluxe has diced tomatoes and onions, too.

My fingers sink into the dough as I spread it out on the pan and it shrinks back. I press my palms into it, feeling the cool stickiness sliding apart under my hands. Making pizza always clears my head. There's nothing to think about, you just follow the instructions. No decisions, no potential screwups—just make it like you're supposed to and it works out.

I need something simple.

Something with instructions.

Something that will work out.

I finish piling on the toppings and slide the pan into the oven just as Gretchen comes around the corner. "You have another table." She nods toward the door. "I gave them menus."

She still seems mad—or at least put off—about me lying to her and saying I was sick. She must've been the perfect eighteen-year-old mom. I could be too if my family was normal and helped out. Of course, if my family was normal, I wouldn't have Addy anyway.

I cringe when I see that my table is three high school kids. Two guys and a girl. They don't tip any better than old people. "Hi," I say, "what can I get you?"

"We'll take a large plain pizza and water," one of the guys says, and shoves the three menus across the table at me.

"I want—" the girl starts to say.

"You don't want anything," the boy beside her says. "Shut up."

Shocked, I take the order to Gretchen and fill up a pitcher of water so I'm not running to the table every three minutes to give them refills, since they're not paying for it. When I get to the table, the shut-up guy and the girl are gone. On my way back to the waitress station, I see them standing in the hallway by the restroom doors.

The boy's gripping the girl's arms and shoving her into the wall. He's saying something I can't make out—it's low and sounds like a growl.

This asshole thinks he can come in here and rough up his girlfriend? No way. I don't think so.

I'm seething with rage. Why's she with a guy like that? I've never understood how girls can let guys treat them like shit and not stand up for themselves.

If she won't, then I will.

He needs to be taught a lesson.

I wait until they're seated back at their table before strolling over to them. "Is there a problem?" I ask, drilling my eyes into shut-up guy.

"I don't have a problem," he says. "Do you?"

My hands clench into fists. "Yeah. I have a big problem. We don't like it when a guy shoves his girlfriend into a wall. It's not something we like our customers doing."

He snorts and points his thumb at the girl. "This slut's not my girlfriend."

Before my mind even registers what I'm doing, I have the pitcher of water over his head and dump it. "I think you need to cool off, tough guy."

"What the hell?" he yells, jumping up.

I slam the empty pitcher back onto the table. "Get out."

"What about my pizza?" he says.

"Get. Out," I say. "And you"—I take the girl's arm—"why are you hanging out with this asshole? You don't deserve to be treated like that." I pivot on my heel and storm away. When I turn back, the three of them are gone.

"What was that about?" Gretchen asks, coming out of the kitchen. She's staring at me with one hand on her hip.

I'm so getting fired.

She's already pissed at me.

I screwed up again.

"That kid pushed his girlfriend into the wall back by the bathrooms. I let him know treating her like that wasn't appreciated."

She lifts her chin and smiles wide. "Good. I think we can live without their five-dollar pizza order, anyway. I like the way you handled it. The jerk looked like a drowned rat." She laughs.

"I hope that girl stops going out with him."

She picks up a fork and a knife and starts rolling them in a napkin. "You gave her something to think about, that's for sure—showed her how to stand up to him."

"Yeah." I feel good, strong. Independent. I have a job, a babysitter I found myself, and the courage to stand up for people like that girl.

I'm really doing it.

I'm making my own life.

I'm making Addy a life.

By the end of the night, I've got eighteen dollars. I love working at Mariani's, but at four sixty-five an hour plus tips, if I don't make more money than this, I don't know if I can stay here long.

• • •

Janine's cat crosses through my headlight beams as I pull into her driveway. I get out of the car and take a deep breath of the dew-damp air. It smells like fresh-cut grass and green leaves. I stretch my arms over my head and look up at the three-quarter moon. I feel like I could float right up beside it, I'm so happy. Everything's working out.

It looks like every downstairs light in the house is on. Janine answers the door with a laundry basket under one arm and the phone in her other hand. "Hang on," she says into the phone. "Hey! She was just an angel." She steps back to let me inside.

Cartoons are blaring on the TV, her little Chihuahua-like dog is jumping on my shins and barking like mad, and toys are scattered everywhere. It's chaos. "Where's Addy?"

"They're just in here," Janine says, leading me into the family room.

But it's empty. No Emma. No Addy.

"Emma Jean!" Janine yells. "Where are you?"

Emma creeps out of the dark dining room into the light of the family room. She's covered in pink and yellow highlighter from head to toe. "Hi," she says to me, waving her little hand. "We're playing fairies."

"Where's Addy?" I ask, trying to swallow the panic that's rushing up my throat.

Janine's already in the dining room flicking on the light over the table. "Emma Jean, where's the baby?"

Emma points under the table. I bend and peer between the chairs. She's lying under there on her back. Every visible inch of her is colored black and green.

"She's the evil swamp fairy," Emma says. "I'm the flower fairy." She puts her arms over her head, the tips of her fingers meeting, and spins like a ballerina. "I caught her and put her in jail."

Janine has a chair pulled out and is on her hands and knees under the table, retrieving my baby. "You leave them alone for one minute to get a load of clothes out of the dryer, and look what happens."

I have no idea why Addy's not asleep, and I can't believe she's not crying. Her eyes are glued to Emma like they're co-conspirators in this game. I guess if she's okay with it, I'm okay with it.

"Let's take her in the bathroom and wash her up," Janine says.

"That's okay. It'll only take a second to get home. I'll scrub up my swamp fairy there and get her jammies on her."

"The markers are washable," Emma says. "I do this all the time." She spins in another circle, with her blond curls trailing behind her through the air. Addy reaches out almost as if she's trying to catch Emma's hair.

"It looks like a fun game."

"Bye, Addy," Emma says, taking Addy's hand and kissing it. "Tomorrow you can be the flower fairy."

My insides melt.

Addy has a friend who lives down the street.

Addy has a home with people who love her.

I'm giving her what she deserves.

chapter

sixteen

It's the first time I've seen Chris's band play, and it's my birthday, but I haven't told him. Because I lied and told him I'm
eighteen, he would think I'm turning nineteen. I'm seventeen,
but feel a lot older, like thirty.

I'm in front of the stage with Jeremy's girlfriend. She's
trashed and can barely stand. She keeps leaning into me and
slurring words I can't make out. The opening band is clearing
their crap from the stage, and house music's blaring from the
massive speakers that are less than ten feet from my head.

I keep telling myself to relax and have fun. This is what
seventeen-year-olds do. They go out and see bands, they get
wasted, they party. Then I remind myself that I have a baby
to take care of.

I have to be responsible.

I chose this.

I chose Addy.

The lights go down, spotlights flick back to life, and Chris and his band come on stage. The crowd goes nuts. The first song they sing is the one he played for me in his room the night I moved in. When he finishes the song, I'm jumping up and down like everyone else.

They play for an hour, and I'm sweaty and high on adrenaline from dancing. Then Chris waits until the crowd calms down and steps back up to the microphone.

"The last song is one I wrote a few days ago. It's for a sweet girl who came into my life and saved me, but she doesn't know it."

He counts his band in and begins to play a slow, beautiful song, accompanied only by a smooth drumbeat. My throat constricts, holding back tears as he sings about holding her in his arms and watching her sleep. It might sound like it's about a woman he loves, but I know it's about Addy.

I can't hold it in any longer, and tears stream down my cheeks. His eyes find me standing below him. They stay locked on mine until the song's finished, and he steps back from the mic to a thunderstorm of applause.

The drummer's girlfriend grabs my arm. "Come on," she slurs, and pulls me backstage.

Chris is sitting on a metal folding chair wiping his face with a towel, his guitar in its case at his feet. My heart thuds like it never has before.

He smiles when he sees me. "Hey."

"Hey." I tuck my hair behind my ear as I approach him.

"What'd you think of my last song?" He pulls me down onto his lap, plunks his grandpa's cap onto my head, and kisses me.

"I loved it. When did you write it?"

"Tuesday night, after you fell asleep. I watched Addy for

about two hours and wrote down everything that came into my head."

I stroke his cheek, then kiss him. "It was the best birthday gift I've ever gotten."

He grabs my shoulders. "It's your birthday?"

I smile sheepishly and nod.

"Why didn't you tell me?"

"I don't know. Just didn't."

"*Leah!* You have to tell me things like birthdays." He stands up, putting me onto my feet, and takes my hand. "Nineteen. You're an old lady."

"How old are you?" The word "jailbait" flits through my head.

"I'll be twenty in September."

Twenty? Whoa.

"We have to find some cake. What's your favorite flavor? Chocolate?" His eyes are excited.

"Cake?"

"Uh, yeah. Birthday cake. Ever hear of it?" He laughs and picks up his guitar case. "See ya," he shouts to his bandmates, waving a hand over his head.

"Later," Aaron says.

I lift my hand and give a quick wave. Being around his friends makes me feel awkward and anxious after the disastrous practice session I bolted out of.

In his pickup, in the parking lot of the local grocery store, we stuff chocolate cake into our mouths, and into each other's mouths.

He kisses me, licking frosting from my lips.

Things have been heating up between us. We've gone beyond kissing when Chris comes upstairs to watch TV at night, and for the first time ever, I don't want to slow them down. I know he's the one. I will be devirginized after all.

Just thinking about it makes me hot and tingly. But there's a big flaw in my plan. He thinks I've had a baby. How can I explain that I'm a virgin? I don't think it's something I can hide.

"Let's go home." I suck frosting from his fingers. "I don't need any more cake."

He kisses me fiercely. "Do you need me?"

I kiss him back, just as fierce. "Soon."

He leans his forehead against mine. "God, I hope it's soon." His laugh's husky and deep like always.

We lie in my bed, under the covers, in nothing but our underwear. Mrs. B insisted on keeping Addy at her house overnight so I could get a night of uninterrupted sleep.

Chris lowers his head and kisses my bare breasts, then lays his head on them. "Leah?"

"Chris?" I stroke his hair.

"I love you." He looks up at me. "I know it's only been a month, but I do. I love you."

If I tell him I love him, I have to come clean. I can't admit to loving someone who doesn't even know my real name. "Are you trying to get me to have sex with you?" I laugh.

He rolls his eyes and lays his head back down. "Maybe." He sounds disappointed. How could he not be, putting his feelings out there and not hearing those words back?

I'm a horrible person. He should hate me.

I tangle my fingers in his hair, intent on keeping him near me. I'll never let go. I'll tell him everything, just not right now.

Gail's picnic table is gouged, and the wood stain faded. We sit across from each other with glasses of sweet tea and a bowl of chips between us. Jonathan rides his red Power Wheels Jeep around the backyard. Addy's inside, where it's cool, napping in her stroller. We left the French doors cracked so we can hear her if she cries.

Gail has her head in her hands, her elbows propped on the table. "I don't know what I'm going to do," she says.

My mind won't focus on anything but the words "I love you" ringing through my head in Chris's voice from last night, but I'm trying to be attentive since Gail has her own issues. "What's going on, Gail?" I pop a chip into my mouth and watch as Jonathan gets dangerously close to crashing his Power Wheels into a tree.

"He doesn't want me." She collapses her arms. Her head falls on top of them.

"Who?" I didn't realize she wasn't over her ex-husband. I'm so not good with this. I have no idea what to say to a woman whose husband has bolted. I can't even remember my own dad leaving.

As if she didn't hear me, she says, "He'll never get over his dead wife."

Picking up my glass, I freeze halfway to my lips. "Huh?" I must have missed something. What the hell are we talking about again?

"I'm in love with him, and he doesn't even want me." She starts sobbing into her arms.

I'm so not good at sympathy. I pat her head. "It's going to be okay. It'll all work out."

"I should've listened to Janine. She said Ken wasn't ready to start seeing someone yet."

"Ken Buckridge? What are you talking about?"

She shakes her head under my palm. "Nothing. I shouldn't have said anything. Just remember, Leah, the truth only screws everything up. I told him I love him, and he hasn't called me in three days."

Yeah. I've got the truth lesson down already.

Later, pushing Addy's stroller home, my mind goes over what Gail revealed to me. Not just that she's dating Mr. Buckridge but that his wife—Chris's mom—is dead.

Truth smacks me in the face. I don't know a lot about the boy I'm falling for, and he knows nothing about me.

That night, after Addy's asleep and Chris and I are practically naked in bed, I run my fingers over his tattoo. One of the dates on the cross is no longer a mystery. Now I have to figure out the other.

"I can't wait to show you something," I tell Chris when he gets home the next night. If I didn't have him to share this with, I would go nuts missing Hope. As it is, I'm dying inside wanting to call and tell her, but I know she wouldn't understand why I'm so excited about it.

"Watch," I say, lifting Add out of the hand-me-down baby swing Gail had given me. I lay her on her stomach on a blanket covering the floor.

She pushes up, puckers her face, shrieks once, and rolls onto her back.

Chris claps his hands. "You rolled over, Squirrel Girl! I'm so proud of you!"

I feel tears start to build in my eyes. He gets it. He's excited with me. "Squirrel Girl?"

"That's what we decided her superhero name would be. Squirrel Girl could communicate with the squirrels and run really fast." He scoops her up and gives her a kiss on the cheek. "You love watching the squirrels, don't you?"

He takes her over to the window. "What a big girl you're

getting to be. Don't grow up too fast, though. I don't want to have to kick boys out of the house yet."

When he's this happy and talks about the future, I feel so guilty, I could die. I know I have to tell him, but I don't know how. The longer I let it go, the harder it is.

He puts her back into her swing and takes me in his arms. "Thank you."

"For what?"

He leans his forehead against mine. "Sharing." He gives me a soft kiss. "I'm going to take a shower. I'll be back up."

When he's gone, I sneak downstairs. Making sure the water's running and he can't hear me from the bathroom, I hurry into his room in search of paper and unearth a song notebook he's clearly forgotten under a pile of old Coke cans and other junk.

Back upstairs, I grab a pen and start writing him a letter—a letter revealing everything.

Dear Chris,

My name is Faith Leah Kurtz. I'm a kidnapper.

I'll spill my guts, but on paper, not out loud. Someday I'll be brave enough to give it to him.

chapter

seventeen

The sky's light, but thunder has been rumbling for the past hour. "Tornado watch until seven," the TV meteorologist says.

Fear darts through me. I hate tornado watches. If it turns into a warning, I'll need to get Addy and take her to the basement—*fast*.

More thunder rumbles. I keep my eyes glued to the TV for weather updates.

The storm is moving in fast. I'm huddled with Addy, wrapped in a blanket. She knows something's coming. She's fussy. Chris is downstairs yakking with his dad like we're not all about to die when the house is blown away. The cheeseburger and fries he picked up for me on his way home from work sit on the table in my kitchenette getting cold and rubbery. I'm too terrified to eat.

Thunder rolls and lightning cracks. I jump about a foot off the couch, and Addy cries. The air feels all wrong, like we're on the verge of something, like someone's picked up the earth and flipped it over. I can't be alone up here one more second. "Chris?" I shout.

The door's shut. He can't hear me.

My feet kick the blanket off of us. I carry Addy over to the door and pull it open.

A whispered argument hits my ears before I can yell for him again.

"Those two up there are not Mom and Kayla. You can't change things. You can't make things right, Chris."

"Dad, I'm not trying to. I know they're not Mom and Kayla. That's not—"

"Chris, I'm not dumb. I see what's going on with you, even if you don't."

Chair legs screech across the floor.

"Don't turn your back on me. I'm still your father. I'm the one—"

"You're the one sleeping with the slut down the street. Yeah. I know."

"Chris, don't you even—"

I close the door fast, but silently. I don't want to hear any more.

Collapsing back onto the couch, I press my hand against my mouth, shocked. What the hell just happened?

I hear footsteps pound up the stairs, and Chris throws the door open. He smiles, but I can tell it's forced. His face is flushed, and he turns from me and walks to the sink, where he leans his hands on the counter and hangs his head.

"Are you okay?" I don't want to let on that I heard what went on between him and his dad, but it's obvious he's upset.

He nods. "It's cool." He takes a deep breath and spins back around, then spies my food, untouched on the table. "Why didn't you eat? Squirrel Girl fussy?" He comes toward me with his arms outstretched. "Here, I'll take her while you eat."

I shake my head, not wanting to let go. Holding Addy is comforting. "I'll eat later. The storm has me freaked out."

His face melts into its natural, warm expression as he drops down beside me and takes Addy and me in his arms. His lips meet the top of my head. "There's nothing to worry about. We have about an hour left until the tornado watch expires."

A flash fills the room, followed by a loud crack. I bury my face in his chest. "I hate that."

"There are worse things than a thunderstorm."

I trace my finger down his chest, over the spot where the cross tattoo hides under his shirt.

Kayla.

That's the other date.

Kayla.

We open my bedroom window to hear the rain. Every now and then a cool breeze blows in and skims across our hot skin.

I love the weight of him on top of me.

I love how our fingers entwine and squeeze.

I love how his slow, deep kisses linger.

"Why won't you let me make love to you, Leah?" he says, pulling his mouth away from my lips and moving on to my ear, where he nibbles.

My entire body is liquid. Hot, boiling liquid. "Is it too soon?" he asks.

I want to shout, *No!* I want him so badly, I might die. I've never wanted anything more in my life.

But instead, I nod. Certain the minute we sleep together

he'll know I'm a liar and it'll all be over. My body aches with deprivation.

He pushes himself up and hovers over me. "Too soon because you're not sure how you feel about me? Or too soon physically because of the baby?"

Holy crap! He just gave me the answer I've been searching for. "I'm afraid it'll hurt."

He smiles, dips, and presses his lips to mine. "But you're sure about us?"

"Very sure." I wrap my arms and legs around him and pull him back down on top of me.

Ten minutes later, I'm tugging his boxer briefs down and begging him to go slow. His hands are reaching over the side of the bed for his pants, trying to get a condom out of his wallet.

The pain isn't unbearable, and he's so gentle, like he's afraid I might break.

After a while, the pace picks up, and I'm wondering if I'm feeling something start to happen—a stirring of heat mingled with the stinging pain.

It's over before I can be sure, and Chris is spent, lying on top of me, kissing my face. "I love you, Leah."

"I love you too." My breathless confession escapes my lips before I can stop it.

He rolls over, pulls me into his arms, and strokes my hair, running his fingers down my back. "God, I'm glad you're here. Both of you."

I'm so relaxed, my mind is blank, but thoughts fade in and out like a slide show.

I'm not a virgin anymore.

I didn't think of my hoebag mom once and push him off.

I want to tell Hope all about tonight. I remember the first time she and Brian had sex. She came home, woke me up, and told me everything. Even what I didn't want to know. God, my heart hurts. It's an ache deep in my chest. I might be dying from missing her.

My palm rests over the dates on Chris's chest. His heart beats steadily underneath.

My letter. I'm a liar. I have to tell him.

He'll hate me.

The in and out of his breathing deepens, and I watch him to make sure he's asleep before scooting out of bed. I tiptoe across the room, grab my robe, and peek into the Pack 'n Play. It's dark, but the moon gives just enough light to see that Addy's forehead's creased, and every once in a while her lips move like she's talking.

Out in the kitchenette, I open the drawer on the far left and take out the notebook with my letter to Chris inside. I flip to a new page and click the pen top.

I was a virgin until tonight. You had no idea, and it kills me. You said you love me, but when you find out the truth, you'll hate me, and I'll still love you forever.

I keep writing while tears smudge the ink. Regret flows through me and onto the pages. Not regret over sleeping with Chris. Never regret over that, and never regret over Addy.

Regret for the lies that cling to me.

Regret I can't shake that just keeps closing in on me.

By the time my hand is cramped and my eyes are burning and begging to close, I've written five more truth-filled pages.

I crawl back into bed. Chris's arm automatically wraps around me, pulling me into his side. I watch him sleep and let tears soak his shoulder.

I can't lose him.

chapter

eighteen

Gail's pushing Addy's stroller. Jonathan is almost a full block ahead of us on his bike, and he still can't brake without crashing into things or people.

I keep going over Chris and his dad's whispered conversation from yesterday again and again in my mind, and I have to have answers. "Gail, what do you know about Chris's mom?"

Gail looks at me. Her eyes are hard, and I think she's going to bitch me out for asking. But she only says, "It's not my place to talk about her," then turns her face forward, watching the sidewalk pass under the stroller's wheels.

I look down at my fingers, picking my nails.

"Chris won't tell you about her?"

I bite my thumbnail. "I haven't asked him. I heard him say something to his dad about her and about dating you."

"Yeah." She sighs. "Ken told me they got into it."

"What else did he say?" My head snaps in her direction.

She frowns. "Ken's worried about Chris . . . and you."

I study the side of Gail's face, wondering if she'll answer the question I really want to know. "Who was Kayla? Did Chris have a sister?"

She frowns and tightens her grip on Addy's stroller. Her fingers turn white. "I think he needs to tell you about his mom and Kayla. I don't think he'd appreciate someone else, especially me, telling you about them."

The rest of the walk to the park is filled with the sounds of birds chirping, lawn mowers whirring, and Gail's stony silence marking the end of our conversation.

Sunday night, we're all sitting around the big oak kitchen table—Chris, Mr. Buckridge, Mrs. B, Ivy, and me.

Mrs. B made spaghetti and meatballs again, just like every other Sunday that I've been here, and I stuffed myself.

Ivy brought brownies for dessert, and Mr. Buckridge is pouring coffee into mugs. Addy's drooling all over Chris's shoulder.

"Oh, I almost forgot," Ivy says, and reaches into her quilted bag to produce a folded newspaper page. "Troy, Viv's son, the firefighter, remember him?" She waits for Mrs. B to nod, acknowledging who Troy and Viv are. "He's on the front page of the paper! Here, look." She unfolds the sheet and smoothes it on the table in front of Mrs. B.

"Viv's our second cousin," Ivy says, reaching across the table and patting my hand. "Her family lives up in Ohio."

I pray my face doesn't reveal my desperation to leave the conversation and run from the room.

I try to smile.

My lips shake.

"Did you know Leah and Addy are from Ohio?" Chris

asks her, pressing Addy over his head, into the air.

"Is that right?" She raises her eyebrows as Mrs. B slides the newspaper page over to Chris.

He lowers Addy and peers over her head at the photo of a fireman in full uniform emerging from a home engulfed in flames.

Chris starts to comment, but I can't hear what he's saying over the loud buzzing in my brain that's triggered when my eyes catch a smaller photo in the bottom right-hand corner of the page.

It's me.

Shit. That's me.

My hand darts out and grabs the page, yanking it from under his gaze. He looks at me like I've lost my mind.

I have. And I'll lose much more than that if he sees the picture of me in the newspaper, staring up at him. "Sorry. Just anxious to look, I guess." I fold the page in half and hold the paper so only the top part is visible.

He laughs. "I guess." And goes back to lifting Addy over his head.

Mrs. B, Mr. Buckridge, and Ivy are chitchatting, but I can feel Ivy's eyes on me and can't flip the paper over to read what's written under my photo.

My God, does she know? Can she blow this whole thing for me and Addy?

Her wrinkled, dry hand grasps the paper and gives it a tug.

Reluctantly, I let go. "A hero in our family, huh?" Ivy says, and laughs as she stuffs the page back into her bag.

I want to dig it out when she's not looking and cram it down the garbage disposal. My stomach rolls. The spaghetti and meatballs threaten to shoot back up. My throat burns with acid.

Chris lifts Addy over his head again, making funny sounds for her.

She laughs for the first time.

His head snaps to me. "Did you hear that?"

I'm so proud of her, my heart swells at the sound. "She laughed!"

I want to cry. I want to bawl like a baby because I'm so happy, and so afraid, and because I know all of this has to end.

My perfect family is a hoax.

I'm a fraud, and this is all a mirage.

After dinner, I'm lying across Chris's lap on the couch upstairs. I ease my hand up his shirt and rub his chest. The room's dark. The TV throws light across his face, then dims.

I'm so comfortable with him. If the newspaper article outs me . . . I have to tell him before that happens. I gather my courage, take a deep breath, and say, "Tell me about your tattoo." It's not my confession. My brain won't work with my mouth, but I want all of his secrets. I want to own this part of him before he's gone from me.

"What about it?" he says, without looking at me.

I lift up his T-shirt and trace the cross with my fingertip. His skin's warm. "What do the dates mean?"

He takes my hand and pulls it to his lips. "They're the dates my mom and sister died."

I sit up on his lap and hold his face in my hands. "I'm sorry."

He smiles. "It's okay." He lifts his shirt again and points to his chest. "It's been two years. I'm over it."

I shake my head. "There's no way you're over it. You never get over losing people you love."

He cocks his head. "Who have you lost?"

I suck in my lips. Nobody. You can't lose people you never had to begin with. But there is Hope. "I haven't lost anyone to death. But I left my sister in Ohio. I miss her." I lift my hair off the back of my neck so he can see my tattoo again. "Hope. That's her name."

I feel his finger running across it. "Too bad your mom didn't name you Faith." He chuckles, and my insides drop to the floor.

I should tell him.

Now is the time to tell him.

There's no way I can tell him.

Addy cries from the other room, sealing the end of our conversation.

"I'll get her," he says, lifting his knees to bounce me off of his lap and onto the couch.

He disappears into my bedroom, and I hear him say, "Hello, little love."

I now know nothing more about his past than I did ten minutes ago, but with those three words to Addy, he's driven himself even deeper into my heart.

The next day at work I'm on edge all day, snapping at customers. The newspaper article perches on my shoulder like my conscience, and the stolen car hunkered in the far corner of the parking lot drives me crazy. I can't wait to get it back in the driveway, hidden in front of Chris's truck.

"Hey," Gretchen says, "since lunch rush is over, come back and help me make lasagna."

This instantly puts me in a good mood. I've been thinking that after they let me start cooking, I could make them the buffalo chicken pizza I invented at Giovanni's—not officially, it was never on the menu or anything—and maybe they'll let me come up with some weekend specials.

Maybe I can even make it to Italy someday. Or go to cooking school. Maybe, twenty years down the road, maybe I can have my own restaurant. Maybe.

I swipe a wet sponge over the counter by the coffeepot and toss it into a bucket of water before finding Gretchen in the kitchen.

I can't ignore the fact that I skipped through the kitchen door, and it makes me paranoid.

"What's wrong?" Gretchen asks, lugging a huge log of provolone cheese out of the cooler.

I shake my head. "Nothing."

Someday I'll stop doubting the good stuff.

Someday the paranoia will be gone for good.

Not today.

When a cop saunters through the door thirty minutes before the end of my shift, I forget to breathe. Sweat trickles down the side of my face, and I wipe it with the back of my hand. He flips through his notepad as he approaches the counter.

"Can I help you?" I croak.

He scoots onto a stool. "Yes. Do you know who owns the Oldsmobile parked in the back corner of the lot?"

I shake my head no and turn toward the kitchen, hoping Gretchen isn't listening.

"Know anybody by the name Faith Kurtz?" He taps his pen on the counter.

"No. Would you like some coffee? Or water?"

The bus boy pushes a cart through the kitchen door and into the dining room. I avoid his gaze. He returns to the back.

"I'm fine," the cop answers. He reaches up to the walkie-talkie hooked to his shoulder, presses the button, and leans his mouth toward it.

I catch the words "stolen vehicle" and "impound."

Shit, shit, shit. How am I going to explain this to Chris? How will I get home?

"Thanks for your help." The cop gets up and leaves.

"What was that about?" Gretchen is behind me. It feels like someone stuffed a concrete block into my chest cavity. "He's towing my car."

"Why?" Gretchen starts rolling silverware.

My mouth goes on autopilot. "Expired plates."

"That sucks. I forgot once, and they only gave me a ticket."

"I'll call Chris for a ride. Mind if I use the phone in the office?" My voice sounds high pitched and shaky.

"Sure. Go ahead. Don't forget to get your car seat before they tow it."

Shit. Car seat. "Thanks."

I sprint out to the parking lot and look around for the cop. He's parked out front by the road. I quickly open the car door and unhook Addy's seat. I know it's snowballing to an end. I can't allow Chris to keep getting deeper and deeper into my lies. He's harboring a fugitive. If I stay any longer, I won't just break his heart, I'll ruin his entire life.

chapter

nineteen

The Fourth of July has always been my favorite holiday. No matter how wasted and bitchy Mom was, the fireworks still exploded in the sky over the lake in the park. She couldn't ruin it or take it away from me.

Even if Santa didn't come on Christmas, the explosions on the Fourth shook me from the inside out, making me forget everything but the water lapping against my legs as I sat on the shore. Sometimes I'd lie back and stare into the sky, and sometimes I'd watch the fireworks drown in the water's reflection.

My favorites are still the gold ones that shoot out in all directions then fall to earth sizzling and crackling.

My house was close enough to the park that I always prayed for one of the fireworks to get a little too close.

To land on the roof.

To spark a fire.

To take my mom away for good.

It never happened.

Of course it didn't, or I wouldn't be in the mess I'm in, sitting here on Mrs. B's patio, eating burgers and potato salad, like I'm not being hunted down by the police for kidnapping and stealing a car.

Chris's arm rests on the back of my lawn chair. His thumb traces circles between my shoulder blades. With every rotation, I hear chanting in my head:

You're a liar.
You're a liar.
You're a liar.

I shift forward, out of his reach. He stands and takes my now-empty paper plate. "Want a brownie? I'm getting one."

"Only one?"

He cracks a smile. "You know me too well. Okay, probably two . . . or three."

"Yeah, grab me one, please."

He goes inside, where platters of food are spread out on the table, leaving me alone with the people who occupy my fake life. Mr. Buckridge sits in a lawn chair against the garage, talking to some old guy. Most of the guests are old. Gretchen stopped by earlier with her little boy but left to take him to see the fireworks. Mrs. B's garden-club members are here, all blue haired and bespectacled. They're all drinking decaf coffee and tugging sweaters over their shoulders despite the ninety-degree heat.

That's what happens, I guess. You go from cutoffs and kegs to cardigans and decaf. I never want to get old.

Mrs. B comes over and sits in Chris's vacant seat. "That baby's made her way around to everyone, I think." She pats my leg. "Edith has her now, took her in to change her diaper."

Old ladies love babies. This is something I've learned in the past couple of months. "She's probably getting tired. She'll be fussing soon." I start to stand, to go inside and find Addy.

"Sit." Mrs. B presses my shoulder down. "She can stay the night here. You and Chris go enjoy the fireworks. I used to love seeing the fireworks with Chris's grandpa. It was so romantic." She gives me a sly smile. "We'd come home and make fireworks of our own." She winks, and I fight off the urge to hurl. The thought enters my mind that she's insinuating that Chris and I will be making fireworks tonight. I'm instantly uncomfortable. Does she know or just assume? There's no way he'd tell his grandma, of all people. I take a deep breath and try to relax.

Chris's hand appears over my shoulder holding a brownie. I take it and look up at him. "Thanks." He's smiling and chewing and has chocolate frosting on his upper lip. It reminds me of my birthday, and I want to lick it off.

He swallows and brushes his hands on his shorts. "Squirrel Girl's asleep. I put her in the Pack 'n Play."

"You're so good with her, dear," Mrs. B says, squeezing his arm and beaming up at him. "Even if you do call her silly names. You'll make a wonderful dad someday."

His face turns crimson, and he avoids my eyes. "Thanks, Grandma."

"Come inside with me for a minute," she tells him, getting up and tugging him by the arm. "We'll be right back out," she calls to me over her shoulder.

My butt's falling asleep from sitting in this chair for so long, and my thighs are sweating against the woven plastic seat. I stand up and run my hands over the back of my legs, feeling the meshlike imprint in my skin.

I walk to the farthest corner of the yard among the

flowering bushes, fragrant lilies, and a small koi pond. Although I've been to Mrs. B's house before, this is my first time in her backyard. It's so different from the dirt and weeds that we called a yard back in Ohio. My feet reach the stones surrounding the tiny pond, and I watch the orange fish dart around underwater. The sun has set, but it's not yet dark. My reflection is like a shadow.

Another shadow reflection appears over my shoulder.

"How's work going, Leah?"

I spin around to face Mr. Buckridge, the man who says approximately three words per day to me. "Hi" and "good night." It's like he has no idea what to say to me.

"It's great. I like it a lot."

"I hear you learned to make the secret Mariani sauce." He stares down into the pond. I turn back around and resume my fish gazing too.

"I did, yeah."

Neither of us speaks for about five minutes, and it's awkward as hell. I'm about to walk away when he clears his throat.

"You know, I was afraid that Chris was getting too attached to you and the baby." He looks at me like he's waiting for my response. "Not because I don't like you or don't want him involved with you, and Addy's a wonderful baby. It's just . . ." He takes a deep breath and shoves his hands into his pockets. "Has he told you about his mom and sister?"

"Umm . . ." I glance back over my shoulder to see if Chris is outside yet. He's not. "He said they both passed away, when I asked him about the tattoo on his chest." I bite my lip and want to be sucked into the ground—I just admitted that I've seen Chris without a shirt. At the very least. God knows what he's thinking now. "That's all he said about it."

He nods and closes his eyes. "After his sister, Kayla, was born two years ago, my wife went into a pretty bad depression . . . this postpartum, baby-blues thing. Then, one morning, Kayla just didn't wake up." He pulls one hand from his pocket and runs it over his face. "Since my wife was already having a hard time, after Kayla died she couldn't take it. Even though she tried counseling and antidepressants, she just turned deeper and deeper inside herself. Shut everyone out." He rocks on his heels and looks up at the darkening horizon. "One day, she slit her wrists. I found her on the bathroom floor when I got home from work." He exhales quickly from his mouth into the sky, like he's releasing demons, and turns his eyes to me. "I just don't want him getting all wrapped up in another woman and baby to have them taken away again."

I feel the tears, see my vision blur, but they won't fall. I won't let them.

He can't see how tortured I am.

He can't know I have to leave soon.

He can't know his son will be hurt again.

"What's going on?" Chris asks, coming up behind me.

"Just watching the fish," his dad says. He pats my shoulder. "Glad you could be here." He walks past Chris and pats his shoulder too. "I'm heading home. I'll see you both   later."

"Later," Chris says.

"Bye," I say. My voice cracks. Chris doesn't notice.

He grips my arms and leads me into a warm, wonderful kiss. The tears finally fall down my cheeks as I close my eyes. And they don't stop.

He pulls back, wipes his cheek, and looks at his hand, then me. "What's wrong? What did he say?"

"Nothing." I let out a shaky laugh. "He didn't say anything. I'm just being dumb." I swipe the tears off my face.

Chris cups the back of my head with his hand. "No.

Something's making you cry. Tell me what it is." He kisses my forehead.

I put my hand on his chest, over the spot where his tattoo is hidden. "He told me about your mom and Kayla."

He leans back to look at me. "What did he tell you? Did he tell you everything?"

I shrug. "I wouldn't know if it *wasn't* everything."

"But, he told you about my mom? *How* she died?"

I nod.

"What about Kayla?"

I blink a few times, contemplating his guarded expression and what it means. "He said she just didn't wake up one morning."

He takes a deep breath, sucks in his lips, and looks over my shoulder, toward the bushes.

"Chris?" I wait until his eyes meet mine again. "Is that why you help me and Addy? That's why you try to keep us safe?"

He doesn't answer, just wraps me in his arms and holds me so tight to his chest, I can barely breathe. "I love you," he says into my hair.

"I love you too," I whisper into his chest, feeling like a traitor. Hating myself more than he ever will. I'm aching inside so badly, I wonder if this is how his mother felt. I don't know what I'll do when I no longer have him in my life.

We're sitting in the middle of a field, side by side on the hood of Chris's truck. There are no other cars or people around. It's just us. Chris has his guitar, and the notes he picks sound hollow and desolate, echoing through the silence.

"Don't people around here come out to watch fireworks?" I lean back, propped on my hands.

"Most of them go to the town square. I come out here. I'd

rather watch them alone. Is that pathetic?" He turns his head and looks at me, then strums his guitar.

I lean back onto my elbows. "No. I always find a spot by myself too. There's something about fireworks—they make you lonely, but good lonely."

We're close enough that I can see his eyes even though it's pitch black. They're intense, probing mine. "Exactly," he whispers. "You get me, Leah."

He grasps my chin with his thumb and index finger and leads my face to his, where our lips meet. His kisses are so delicate and sweet. He cherishes me. I can feel it in his kiss.

He leans his forehead against mine. "My grandma wanted me to go inside with her so she could give me something. She's hoping I'll give it to you someday. I know I will. I know I want you to wear it for the rest of your life."

My entire body goes numb. Is he talking about what I think he's talking about? Did she give him her ring?

If that wasn't clear enough, he takes my left hand and kisses my ring finger.

Holy shit.

Before I get my heart and mind back in sync, there's a deafening boom, and reflected in his eyes I see the brilliant sparks of multicolored fireworks.

I can't deny how I feel about him. I love him. I want that ring someday. I want to be his wife. I want him to be Addy's father.

If I keep her that long.

If he doesn't hate me when he finds out what I did.

If I don't go to prison for the rest of my life.

His lips find mine again. His hands stroke my face, my legs, my neck. We make love on the hood of his truck, under a sky filled with lonely fireworks.

chapter

twenty

When Chris and I get home from work on Friday night with Addy, we're faced with the shock of a lifetime. Gail and Jonathan are there for dinner.

As soon as Chris sees them sitting at the table eating pizza, he throws his keys against the wall and storms into the kitchen.

He doesn't break his stride. "Dad, I need to talk to you outside." He continues through to the back door that's thrown open as he goes out, the screen door banging against the house.

Ken's pissed. He gets up and follows Chris, taking care to close the door behind him.

I slink into the kitchen and slide onto the chair beside Gail, resting Addy on my shoulder. "How did this happen?" I gesture to the pizza.

She shakes her head. "I don't know. He called late last night and told me he's tired of being alone. He said he's ready to move on with his life. Then he asked me to come over with Jonathan for pizza tonight."

"Hmm." I force a smile. I'm happy for her but devastated for Chris. Ken might be ready to move on, but Chris isn't ready for him to forget his mom.

"Chris is pissed, huh?" she asks.

I grimace. "What gave you that idea?" I lean back in my chair. "Ken's pissed too," I say.

She nods. "What a mess."

Outside, their voices rise, making it possible for us to hear them inside. "Jonathan"—I stand and walk round the table—"come upstairs and watch TV with me and Addy, okay?" Chris and Ken's fight has even shocked Jonathan into stone stillness. I've never seen him like this.

"I'm coming too." Gail jumps from her chair.

We hurry Jonathan up the stairs and get him situated with some cartoons. Just as I sit down with Addy and a bottle, I hear the back door slam.

"Want me to take her?" Gail asks, knowing I want to go to Chris.

I nod and hand Addy over. "I'll be right back."

I open the door and listen before creeping down the steps. It's silent. Ken is sitting in his spot at the kitchen table, staring at the ceiling.

"Want me to tell Gail you're back inside?" I ask.

"She upstairs?"

"Yeah."

He sighs and pushes his chair out. "I'll go up. We'll go to her house." Before he climbs the steps, he pauses. "Talk to him. He needs someone to listen. It can't be me now. He doesn't want it to be me anymore." His shoulders slump. I've never seen him as sad.

I don't see Chris. His keys are on the floor by the coffee table. I pick them up and head down the hall to his room. The door's shut, so I knock. When there's no answer, I open it.

He's lying on his bed with his back to the door. "Hey." I ease into the room and shut the door behind me. "Are you okay?" I sit down and put my hand on his head, stroking his hair. "Talk to me."

He shakes his head and doesn't say anything. I lie behind him and drape my arm over him. We lie in silence for what seems like forever.

"Did you know?" It's almost a whisper.

"Did I know?" I sit up, and he rolls onto his back.

"Did you know about her and my dad?"

I'm not sure why it matters if I knew. "She's mentioned your dad before."

His face draws tight. He's so mad, it looks like he could open his mouth and a deep, fierce growl would echo from his throat. "You never said anything."

"I didn't know it's a big deal that your dad is seeing her." I rest my hand on his arm, and he shrugs it off and sits up on the edge of the bed with his back to me. "Chris . . ."

"Just . . . don't. I need to think. I have practice. I'll talk to you later." He grabs his guitar case and his cap and bolts from the room. Squeezing his keys, which are still in my hand, I lean against the headboard and wait.

The front door opens and closes.

I know he'll be back.

The front door opens and closes.

He's back.

I dangle his keys from my finger. "Looking for these?"

"Yeah." He reaches out to snatch them, and I wrap my fingers around them, keeping them tight in my fist.

"You're not getting them until you talk to me."

He runs his hands over his face in frustration. "I'm late already, Leah. Just give me my keys."

I shake my head. "No. Sorry."

"I'm serious!" he shouts.

"So am I!" I shout back.

He dives at me, landing on the bed, half on top of me, half off. We wrestle for the keys. He grabs my wrist and tries to pry my fingers open. I kick and squirm and pull my arm free. We're both irritated with each other, and we're blowing off steam.

I can't help it. This is so ridiculous that I start giggling. That only makes him angrier.

He takes both of my wrists and pins them beside my head. "This is funny to you? My dad's dating her. Do you think it's cool if he forgets about my mom?"

"No, that's not—"

"I can't believe you. I don't know you at all." His eyes drill into mine. I know he's hurting. I know he doesn't mean it, but his words sting. They're the words I've heard him say to me in my head a million times.

I'm a bitch.

A lying bitch.

I open my hand, revealing the keys.

He takes them and heads toward the door. He pauses and looks back over his shoulder. "We'll talk later," he mumbles, then leaves.

I have this heavy blanket of sadness wrapped around me. When he gets home, I want things to be back to normal. I don't want to talk. I don't want any of *that* to ever have happened.

Addy's asleep. My notebook and pen sit on the table in front of me. I've written until my eyes crossed. I've spilled everything about my life. I've told him about my mom, about Hope, about Addy. Everything. I've even told him how much I love him and how much I want to be with him, wearing his grandma's ring.

My head's pounding.

My eyes are raw.

My hand's cramped.

I hear footsteps on the stairs. I dash across the kitchen and toss the notebook and pen into the drawer. He knocks. I tighten the belt on my robe and open the door.

He smiles, but it's small and weak.

I cross the room and collapse onto the couch. He sits beside me.

"I'm sorry," he says. "I didn't mean it."

"Okay."

"I was mad that you didn't tell me when she told you about my dad."

"Are you still?"

"A little."

"What was I supposed to say that you didn't already know? If you wanted to talk to me about it, you would've. Why would I bring it up?" I cross my arms over my chest.

"I know. You're right."

"Do you want to talk about it?"

He shakes his head and pulls me to him. "No. I don't want to waste time talking about them. I'd rather think about us." He kisses me quickly, testing the water. "How's Add?"

"Sleeping."

"Good. She's been sleeping well lately."

I nod.

"You're still upset with me."

I shrug.

He takes my hand, stands, and pulls me up. "Come on. Let me give you a massage to make it up to you." He tugs me into the bedroom and makes me lie on the bed on my stomach. I feel his weight on my rear as he straddles me and sits down on top of me.

His hands press and knead my shoulders. It feels so good, I could lie here for days. "I hate to fight," I say into the pillow.

He rises to his knees, scoops me into his arms, and flips me over. "Now comes the fun part. Making up."

So we do. Twice. Before we fall asleep, I slip out of bed. "I have something to show you."

Inside Addy's baby bag, I find the picture of me, Mom, and Hope. I take it back to bed and hand it to Chris.

He scoots up against the headboard and studies it. "Hope and your mom?"

I nod and lean against his shoulder.

"You were young here. How old?"

"Eleven. That was during a very brief time when my mom wasn't drinking or doing drugs."

"You look like her."

I hold my fist up over his crotch. "You want to lose your manhood right here and now, don't you."

He grabs my hand. "You look nothing like her. That's what I meant to say." He kisses my knuckles and turns back to the picture. "Addy looks a little like Hope."

I snuggle into him. "I know."

"Does Addy look like her dad?" He glances toward the Pack 'n Play.

"She gets her coloring from him." It's not a lie.

"Was he there when she was born?"

"No." Another truthful answer. Just not exactly answering the question he's asking.

"Who was there with you? Your mom?"

"Yeah, she was there." Couldn't have happened without her.

He rolls toward me and pushes my hair back off my face. "Would you ever do it again?"

I close my eyes and exhale. "Yes. Someday I'll do it."

His kiss brushes my lips before he pulls me into his arms and falls asleep.

Work's a waste the next day. It's rainy, and the dining room's empty. Chris brought me in, along with a dozen gallons of Mrs. B's sauce, which I helped her make. Now he's in the back chatting with Gretchen. He keeps offering to pay to get my car out of the impound lot. I keep telling him I want to save the money myself. This is buying me some time.

Not that there will ever be enough time. Eventually, I'll have to tell him that the car's not mine. That Addy's not mine.

I shove the Bissell carpet sweeper under a table where three little kids had just been sitting. No matter how many times I run the vacuum over the pile of Goldfish crackers, they won't all sweep up. They left me a buck. Jerks.

The bell above the door jingles, alerting me to a customer. I turn and look.

It's the cop.

This time he has a photo in his hand.

I drop to the floor, praying he didn't see me, and crawl to the ladies' room on my hands and knees.

I hear him calling "Hello?" at the counter.

Chris's muffled voice answers a few seconds later.

The cop's going to show him my picture.

He's going to know.

He's going to know my name's Faith.

He's going to know I kidnapped Addy and stole Mom's car.

I start gagging and run to the toilet. I throw up and keep gagging. I'm going to lose him. I'm going to lose Addy. It's happening.

The bell above the door jingles again. I peek out and don't see the cop or Chris. I take a few steps and straighten my apron.

"Ahem," Chris coughs behind me. "We need to talk."

I'm screwed.

I follow him back out front. He sits at the counter, and I go around to face him. "What did the cop want?"

He raises his eyebrows. "He had a picture of you. Want to tell me why he's looking for you?"

"He didn't say?" Hope blooms in my chest.

"No, and I didn't tell him you were here." He knocks on the counter. "It's your ex, isn't it? Addy's dad. Is he looking for her?"

He has to stop doing this. Before I even get into a corner, he has me back out again and puts himself there instead. He just keeps bailing me out, feeding me excuses.

"I think so." A light comes on in my head. "I can't get the car back, Chris. It's in his name. He let me drive it, but I don't have the registration."

He nods, closes his eyes, and sighs. "Why didn't you just tell me that?"

"I didn't want you to know the cops were looking for me."

He takes both my hands across the counter. "I love you, Leah. We're in this together."

I lean on my elbows and kiss his hands. "I have to go back," I whisper.

"Go back?"

"I have to go back home to Ohio. I can't stay. Everything's a mess."

He yanks my hands, making me look up into his eyes. "You're not leaving. You can't go back."

"I can't be with you with all of this going on. It's not fair to you. You have no idea."

Tears stream down my face now, and his eyes are wet. "You aren't leaving me. You're not taking Addy from me."

I take his face in my hands and kiss him gently. "I have to go back and fix this. It's time. They found me."

He shakes his head. "Not without me. I'll take you wherever you want to go, but I'm going with you. Then we're coming back home." The fierce look on his face tells me he's not going to waver on this.

I'll have to figure something out. For now, I nod. "Okay."

Before I leave the restaurant that night, I tell Gretchen I can't work anymore and feed her the same lie I told Chris. My entire life is a huge lie.

I can't live like this anymore.

chapter

twenty-one

The heat is sweltering inside the phone booth at the gas station. My sweaty hand clutches the handle of Addy's stroller, which is parked right outside the phone-booth door. She's belting out high-pitched squeals that could wake the dead.

The kid's got some pipes.

I dig in the pocket of my shorts with my free hand for the pile of quarters I've been saving from my tips the past week. I know I have to make this phone call. I have to see how bad it is at home before plunging back in.

I plunk each coin into the slot, hearing it land with a hollow clunk inside the phone. Who knows how many it'll take to call Ohio from a pay phone, but judging by the weight of the quarter stash in my pocket, I should be able to call China.

Needing my right hand to dial, I release Addy's stroller and wipe my sweaty palm on my shirt before jabbing in her cell phone number as fast as I can. No second thoughts—just do it and get it over with.

She answers on the third ring. "Hello?"

I swallow.

My hand is shaking, making the receiver slide around against my ear. "Hope?"

Silence.

Then she clears her throat.

"What do you want?"

She's not mean exactly, just monotone, suspicious.

"I'm coming home soon."

"I can't believe you did this. Mom is *so* pissed!"

"I know. Do you think I should call her? Before I come back, I mean?" I suck in my lips and jiggle the phone cord.

"Listen, I'm not involved in this. I told *her* that, and I'm telling *you* that. I'm at Ohio State. I have a life. I don't want my old one back. Do you know you're in the newspaper? Do you know how embarrassing that is?"

"But, Hope, what do you think I should do?"

"Turn back time and, let's see . . . *not* steal the baby?"

"Okay, given that turning back time isn't really an option, what else?"

"I don't know, Faith. I've got to get to the track."

There's a click, followed by a dial tone.

I place the receiver on its cradle and push my hair back from my sticky face. My stomach hurts like hell.

Hope hung up on me.

She's done with me.

I'm totally alone.

I shove the glass door open, bend over, and gag. I choke and spit. Tears stream from my eyes. My nose runs.

Between the *whoosh* of cars rushing by, there's the sound of sobs—my sobs. I haven't heard myself bawling since middle school, and it makes me want to kick something.

My hands swipe across my eyes. I grit my teeth, pound my fists against my thighs, and scream.

I can't believe Hope won't help me!

I dig in the bag under the stroller and pull out my Happy Place picture. My thumb runs over Hope's face. My lips tighten and shake. "You suck, Hope! You suck!" I yell, tearing the picture into a million tiny pieces and tossing them to the wind. I watch as they drift into the road and get lost under the tires of an eighteen-wheeler flying by.

Thick tears drip onto the front of my T-shirt. I sniffle and blink like crazy, shake my shoulders, and take deep breaths. Screw them. I've gotten this far. I'll figure this out by myself. I blow all the air out of my lungs and take hold of the stroller. "I don't want to go back there, Add."

I push her through the gas station parking lot, back to the sidewalk.

I can't imagine pulling up to that house—where there's no food, random men roaming in and out, and always a drunk, crazy woman to deal with—and getting out with the baby. I can't imagine—don't want to imagine—the look on my mom's face.

The things she'll say.

Giving over Addy.

Letting them wreck her, too.

I let my head fall back and close my eyes. The sun's bright behind my eyelids, swallowing me in an orange glow.

I almost don't notice the music drifting into my ears.

It sounds like an ice cream truck jingle.

I search around, thinking a Popsicle with a gumball stuck in the top sounds like a good plan for my leftover quarters.

Then I realize the music's coming from Addy's stroller.

I let go of the handles and walk around to peer in. She's stretching her arm up toward a toy cat dangling from the stroller's hood.

Her face is one big ball of concentration—her forehead crinkled, eyes focused, jaw taut. Her arm wavers, fingers splayed, determined to reach the pink plastic cat and make the music play again.

She bats it, and it goes off. She pulls her arm in and sucks on her hand.

"That's right, Add, lie back and relax. You earned it." I lean in and rub her soft head, then kiss her cheek.

My eyes blur with more tears.

She's all I've ever had.

This is a dumb thought, and I know it. I never expected to keep her forever, did I?

Maybe I did.

On the way home, I mentally catalog everything I've lost:

My dad. I have a vague memory of him from when I was really little, like maybe three. We're sitting on a couch somewhere. A TV's on, NASCAR, I think. The memory carries the distinct sour smell of beer and B.O. I want to say that he read me a book at bedtime, but I might be making that part up.

Shithead. A stray wiener dog my mom brought home once. She named him. He slept with me and chewed a hole in my Holly Hobbie comforter. Even though we'd gotten it at Goodwill, Mom beat him with her shoe and threw him outside. He ran away.

Frank. That boyfriend of Mom's who hung around for about a year when I was in middle school. In addition to taking us on our one family vacation ever, he taught me how to play basketball and even got me onto a team at the Y. He came to every game. Then mom got stoned and fucked that up too.

Friends. I had one once. In first grade. Her name was Heidi. She had long blond hair that she wore in two braids on the sides of her head. Her front teeth were missing, and she carried a Barbie backpack. One day, I rode the bus home with her. My mom forgot to pick me up. When Heidi's mom drove me back to my house, my mom was passed out on the front steps. That was the last day Heidi was allowed to be friends with me.

I don't know if you could say I lost Mom. She was never really mine to begin with, outside of being the DNA donor and incubator for forty weeks. But when I looked at the picture of us—her, me, and Hope standing in the surf—I could still feel her thin arm resting around my shoulders. I could hear her laughing clear and loud when the waves rushed up our calves and we stumbled in the surf, holding on to each other.

But Hope. My heart twists and throbs at her words. I'm an embarrassment to her. Just like Mom's always been to me. I'm just like Mom.

"Just a few more weeks?" Chris strokes my arm. His chest is bare, and his hair is tousled from sleep. Addy's gurgling in her swing in front of the TV, and I'm getting Chris and me bowls of cereal for breakfast. He pulls me into his arms and tucks my head into his chest.

He's warm. I could fall back to sleep standing here with my face pressed against his skin. I curl my toes over the tops of his. "I'll think about it."

He's been begging and pleading with me to stay just a little longer. It's almost impossible to even think about saying no to him without breaking down into blubbering, pathetic mush, but my call to Hope yesterday put the situation into perspective—I can't hide out anymore. I have to fix things. I haven't really escaped at all until I tell Chris everything and this running and hiding is over.

"I've been thinking." Chris runs a hand over my head, getting his fingers stuck in my tangled morning hair. "He'll probably just give up. The cops haven't found you. They'll move on, and he'll give up." His lips press against the top of my head.

"Yeah, maybe." I know he doesn't really believe this, so there's no reason to argue about it. Plus, it's a lie. What's there to argue? It is what I make it.

He takes a deep breath. "Leah, I got a job offer. To fix guitars."

I pull away to see his face. "You did?" I hear the sob in my throat lurch out, without knowing it was coming. It's his dream.

He pulls me back to his chest. "Manny, the guy who owns the bar in Jacksonville where we play sometimes, put me in contact with the owner of Ley's Guitar Shop there. They're going to let me start when we get home from Ohio." His thumb trails over my cheek. "Ley's is, like, internationally known. They've even done work for Joe Walsh."

He has an offer for his dream job, where he'll be working after I'm gone and he's hating me. My dream had started, then got sucked away by my lies. I want to die.

"Since Jacksonville's an hour and a half away from here, I thought maybe we could get an apartment there. Is that okay with you? If we live together? Me, you, and Addy?"

He wants to live with me.

He's going to hate me.

I'm going to lose him.

chapter

twenty-two

On Saturday, while Chris is working at his roofing job, Addy and I hit the neighborhood-wide yard sales that are going on. Mrs. B and Ivy are using Ken's house as a base for selling their own junk. I left them organizing their stuff on picnic-table benches in the front yard.

The five bucks in my pocket is a fortune in old-junk-buying terms. Addy's getting so long, the snaps on her clothes hardly fasten between her legs anymore. Hopefully we can find some baby clothes.

I get to Gail's and freeze in my tracks. It appears as though her entire house has been turned inside out, with its contents strewn all over the lawn and haphazardly set out on tables. In the center of the chaos, I see her bent down between two boxes, her red bandanna wound around her head.

"Hey! Gail!" I push the stroller up her driveway. "You've got a lot of stuff here."

"Well . . ." She swipes her brow with her forearm and looks around. "Yeah. Guess I do. Years of accumulated shit from a shit marriage." She slumps down in a lawn chair. "I won't need all of this when Jonathan and I move out. Just hope the house sells fast."

"Whoa. Wait. You're selling your house? Why?" My eyes run over the five-bedroom Tudor-style home. I've never lived in anything even half as nice.

Except now.

Now I live in a nice family home.

Now won't last forever, though, only a few more days.

She shrugs. There's a gleam in her eye. "I just won't need my own house anymore." She can't resist the smile that tugs at her lips.

My chin drops. "You're not moving into Ken's when I leave?"

She nods, giggling and smiling. "Yes! That's our plan. He said you and Chris are getting your own place in Jacksonville after you get back from Ohio, so we can make the upstairs a huge bedroom and playroom for Jonathan." She claps her hands together. The sound smashes something inside my brain every time her hands ricochet off of one another.

This is not happening.

Chris is going to shit bricks.

I have to tell him—he'll flip out if I keep this from him.

"Are you two getting married?"

She shakes her head and starts picking at her shoe. "No. He's adamant about that. He will only ever have one wife."

Addy starts blowing raspberries. I push her back and forth in the stroller. "And you're okay with that?"

She stands, pulls a stack of old CDs out of a box, and starts sorting through them. "Yeah, you know. Whatever." She tosses one back in the box. "It is what it is. I can accept it or not." Her eyes meet mine. "I want him. So I accept it."

I smile. "Sure. I understand. I'm excited for you!" I let go of the stroller and give her a hug.

I'm not excited for me. Chris's head is going to explode when he finds out.

She makes a sweeping motion with her arm. "Go ahead. Look around. Whatever you want, it's yours. Just take it."

"Um, okay. Thanks." I twist my ponytail, observing her piles of *stuff*. I don't even know where to begin. A stack of T-shirts catches my eye, and I head over to them.

Gail's taking Addy out of her stroller.

She must really love Ken. Some people will ignore a lot to be with the person they love.

My hands tug a red blouse from the pile.

I don't know if Chris would ignore what I've done just to be with me. I don't know if I could ask him to ignore it, or to forgive me for lying to him.

I have to stop this.

I hastily fold the red blouse and pick up a brown T-shirt.

Chris can't follow me home. They're going to arrest me as soon as I put one foot on Mom's porch.

Across the road, Janine has Emma's baby clothes hanging on a line. "I'm going to head over and check out Janine's baby stuff. I really am happy for you."

Gail smiles and starts to say something when there's a huge bang from inside. "Jonathan!" she yells, placing Addy into my arms, then jogging off across the yard.

I laugh and shake my head, situate Addy back into her stroller, and push her across the street.

"Hey, Leah." Janine's counting money and stuffing it into a plastic container. "I was hoping you'd stop by. I have a ton of

Emma's stuff to sell." She tilts her head, scrutinizing me. "I'll give you a good deal. I hear you have a situation back home. The least I can do is help with Addy's clothes."

My mouth goes dry. "What kind of situation?" I ask her as she folds all the baby clothes and tucks them into a plastic grocery bag. "What did you hear?"

"I heard that you're in some kind of trouble back home." She ties the handles on the bag together. "You don't have to tell me what you did. I just want to help where I can." She hands me the bag, smiling like the cat that ate the canary.

"Thanks." I'm shaking my head, like she's full of it. "Where did you hear that?"

"Yesterday at church Mrs. B confided in me. The story is that Ivy confirmed with her family in Ohio that you have some issues back home to iron out. I guess it was in the newspaper."

My heart stops.

"Figures," I mumble under my breath, whipping the stroller around and racing down the sidewalk, running out on my conversation with Janine.

Ivy and Mrs. B come into view, sipping lemonade on the front porch steps next to a black cash box while a few shoppers browse through their old treasures. Mrs. B lifts her cold glass and runs it across her forehead. Ivy's fanning herself with her blouse, making it billow with air.

I'm boiling over, from the heat and from anxiety as I shove Addy's stroller up the driveway full speed. I just want to get inside and figure out what to do.

"Leah! Bring that darling baby girl over here!" Ivy calls.

"I need to change her first. I'll bring her back out." Like hell I will. I keep barreling toward the back patio.

When I get inside the house, it's cool and silent, but my

head's still running in lopsided circles like our washer back home when it got unbalanced.

I have to leave. Ivy, or Mrs. B, could've called the cops. They might show up any second and take Addy away and me to prison, or a detention home somewhere for minors.

My feet pound up the stairs. The air dries the sweat on my body, making me sticky. I need a shower, but there's no time.

I have to pack.

I have to finish my letter.

I have to leave.

I don't make it. Chris comes home before I get the letter finished, but I've packed our bags and hidden them under my bed until I can tell him I'm leaving.

He knocks and opens the door. Since I heard him coming, I'm sitting on the couch holding Addy as she practices standing up on my legs, the letter stashed in a drawer. She can keep herself up for a few seconds before her knees buckle. He swoops over and gives us both a kiss.

"How are my girls? Find her any clothes?" His smile's so bright. Eyes so happy-Chris-blue. It blackens my heart knowing I'll wipe that smile off of his face for good.

"I got quite a few things." Gail flashes into my mind. I can't tell him about Gail moving in and then leave. There's no freaking way I'm bearing that news too. He grabs my hand. "I have the best night planned for us. Grandma's watching the baby, and I'm taking you out. Before we leave to take you home, I just want one more perfect night with you here."

His lips kiss each of my fingertips.

My lips find the corner of his mouth, his cheek, his neck.

My life won't ever be right without Chris in it.

• • •

Two hours later, we're sitting in a booth in a steak house, picking at our salads, when he pulls out his wallet and hands me three hundred dollars. He doesn't say a word, just hands it to me.

My hand shakes holding the bills. "What's this?"

He rolls his eyes. "Do you really think I could take rent from you? I was going to open an account for Addy with it, but since you can't work at the restaurant anymore because of the cop . . ."

My shoulders sag. I have no defenses against him. "I want to go home," I whisper. A tear trickles down my face.

He comes to my side of the booth and scoots in beside me. "What's wrong?" His thumb wipes the tear away.

"Nothing. I never knew a person could be so perfect. I want to go home with you. I don't want to be here wasting time. Let's just go home and go to bed."

I need to be close to him.

I need to feel him against me.

I need to remember how it feels forever.

But he just laughs and squeezes my thigh. "We'll get there. Let's enjoy all of tonight."

Next on his list is a moonlit walk around the pond in the park. We throw hunks of our leftover bread from dinner to the geese so they don't riot on us. Chris has a plastic bag with him. I don't know what's in it. He leads me by the hand over to a picnic table and pulls out a bottle of wine and a plastic container of strawberries. The wine has a twist top, and we take turns chugging it from the bottle. Then we feed each other strawberries, licking the juice from each other's fingers and lips, like the cake on the night of my birthday.

Soon, we're tipsy and running around the playground. He follows me down the slide. We land in a heap at the bottom, where we roll around in the mulch, laughing our asses off. I hear my voice echoing through the dark night, and I know I've never laughed like this before.

"I don't want this to end!" I scream to the moon.

"It doesn't have to," Chris says, pulling me across the mulch, into his arms. "We can have this much fun no matter where we are. Even in Ohio."

God, he doesn't get it. *I won't be with you!* I want to scream. *I'll be detained somewhere! Addy will be taken from us!*

Before my mind can drag itself down deeper, Chris's hands begin to work frantically, removing my clothes, so my hands do the same in return.

"I love you, Leah!" he yells to the moon, as loudly as I had screamed before.

It sounds like he means it, like he does love me and won't ever stop.

But I know better.

It comes to me in the middle of the night, like all the best ideas do. With Chris sleeping in my bed, I slide his wallet out of his jeans, which lie in a heap on the floor. Then I sneak downstairs to his room, boot up his computer, and get online. I figure we'll leave here in the evening tomorrow so Addy will sleep for about six hours. Then we'll have to stop.

I pull up a map and find the city off of the highway, six hours north of here, right outside Atlanta. Then I find the closest airport and click on ticket information. I purchase a one-way ticket back to Akron on Chris's credit card and leave a hundred and fifty bucks in rent money under his keyboard to pay him back.

Before I click off of the page, I notice the words "airport shuttle," and jot down the phone number. Wherever we are when I ditch Chris, we'll have a ride to the airport.

chapter

twenty-
three

Chris is sullen. That's a good word for it. Sullen. And brood-
ing. It's like he knows I snuck out of bed last night and bought
a plane ticket—plotted leaving him.

"I don't want to have a confrontation with your ex," he
says over breakfast, stabbing a forkful of scrambled eggs.
When we came to pick up Addy this morning, Mrs. B made
us stay, and she's cooking us breakfast.

Mrs. B glances at me from the stove, manning a pan of
spitting bacon. "Chris is going back with you to straighten
out a *situation* with your ex?"

Oh, God, she knows the truth, and she knows I'm lying
about it to Chris. I prop my elbows on the table and hide my
face in my hands. "It's . . . complicated."

If only it were an ex that has me fleeing from the best place
I've ever been, with an almost family.

"If it's complicated, maybe it's best if Chris stays here until you have it worked out." Her voice sounds desperate. She wants me out of his life. I can't blame her.

My arms collapse, and my head lands on top of them. "Maybe."

"No," Chris says, and pounds his fist on the table. "I'm going with you."

I glance up. Mrs. B has her hand on Chris's shoulder. His head's dropped down, chin to chest. Her eyes meet mine. "Hurry and get things straightened out so you both can come home to us with my baby girl." Her eyes are hard. She squeezes his shoulder.

Oh my God, my heart hurts so bad, I think I'm having an attack.

Chris and I are lying on our backs, side by side on my bed as Addy naps in her Pack 'n Play. My right leg is slung over his left, my hand in his. He rolls to his side and whispers in my ear. "I know about the newspaper article."

I suck in my lips and squeeze my eyes closed. "What does it say?"

"That you disappeared with a baby." He rises on his elbow to see my face. "But I knew that."

I focus on the ceiling. "Anything else?"

His fingers find my jaw, and he turns my face toward his. "That's all it said. *Is* there something else?"

I wrap my arms around him and roll him onto his back so I can rest my head on his chest. I want to hear the thumping of his heart—memorize the sound of it beating. But I don't answer him. No more lies.

"Four hours until we leave," he says, picking up strands of my hair and breathing it in. "I should pack the truck. Do you have everything ready to go?"

I nod into his chest. "Just need to grab some of Addy's things that I left out, and pack up the diaper bag."

His hands push against my shoulders to roll me off of him.

"No, not yet. We have time." My fingers entwine with his, and I make him lie back again.

We fall asleep, and I don't dream.

While Chris packs the car, I take Addy for one more trip to the park. It's dusk, and everyone's inside, lounging in front of their TVs or eating dinner.

Lawn sprinklers sprout up from flower beds and shoot jets of water, making a *cht, cht, cht* sound as they circle. The noise drowns out everything else in the world. The wind sends sprinkles of water across my calves, and chills creep up to my thighs.

Addy's quiet. It's eerie. She's not even gurgling like she does all day long now.

I think she knows.

I push the stroller through the entrance to the park, up to the bench beside the wispy little tree near the playground. With the stroller faced toward me, I sit down.

Addy watches me and kicks her feet. Her arms dart above her head. Her movements aren't as jerky as they used to be. She's getting used to living inside her body.

I'm getting used to living with her, too, with her face and eyes, her smiles and giggles.

This is it. The knowledge that this is what I've been dreading gnaws at my stomach. These are our last hours together, as mother and daughter.

My fingers unfasten her belt, and I lift her into my arms. Her hand rests on my cheek, and she laughs.

I cry.

I sob into her pink, polka-dotted romper while she tugs on my hair.

I hold her so close, her cheek is pressed against my eye. Her hands slide through the tears on my face. I can feel the flutter of her tiny heart and remember seeing it beat on the ultrasound monitor.

"I knew then. I had to keep you. Somehow, you were mine."

I look into her eyes, and she looks back. She's silent again and doesn't smile. Her hands stay on my face, feeling the cool, wet tears fall.

"You know, don't you?" I whisper.

She leans forward and lays her forehead against my nose.

"I love you, Add. I love you, baby."

It's so dark, I can't see a thing out the passenger-side window. The truck's headlights shine through the fog but give only a few feet of visibility. Chris is driving slow, so slow that I might miss my flight.

I can't miss my flight.

I can't let him drive me home.

I have to lose him along the way.

My eyes are gritty from crying. They're so heavy, it takes a lot of effort to keep them open.

"Go ahead and sleep," Chris says, patting my leg. "You don't have to keep me company. It's cool."

"I'm okay. Not tired."

He laughs. "Your eyes are all squinty. You can barely keep them open."

"It's just—"

"You've been crying. I know." His arm snakes around my shoulders, and he pulls me closer to kiss my temple. "Everything's going to be okay. I promise."

I shake my head. "You don't know. Don't promise."

"I do know." His smile, ignorant of the truth, affects me more than his words. "And I promise."

Addy sighs and gurgles in her sleep behind us. I reach back and absorb the feel of her downy hair under my fingertips. I can't imagine living without her.

Without baby sighs and gurgles.

Without Chris.

I can't picture myself back at school. Maybe I can get my GED or finish school with some online program. Not that I have a computer. I could fully embrace my future as my mother's daughter and start selling drugs, or sex. Then I could afford a computer. Of course, I wouldn't need to graduate for either of those jobs.

I wonder how much time I'll have to do for kidnapping Addy. I hope they send me away somewhere and don't make me stay at home locked down with one of those ankle bracelets. That would be the worst punishment they could sentence me to.

I flop back against the seat and lean my elbow against the door. This trip is going to fly by because I want it to last forever— just me and my last hours with my two favorite people on the planet.

Chris has a map on the seat between us that I snatch up. I click on the light overhead and study it. "We should stop here." I point at a little town, the one where I plan on ditching him. "Addy will need to be changed and fed by the time we get there."

"Sounds like a plan." He takes the map and sets it back on the seat, then starts fiddling with the radio.

He's so easy, so quick to believe. These traits shouldn't irritate me so much, and probably wouldn't if I wasn't manipulating him.

I hate myself.

There's something about the motion of driving down a highway that lulls me to sleep. I fight it. I don't want to miss one second of this trip. But I find myself opening my eyes as Chris's door slams shut. I've been asleep.

We're at a gas station. I glance at the clock on the dashboard— it's been two hours since I was last aware of the time. We should be close.

I climb out of the truck and round the truck bed to where Chris is standing with his hands shoved in his pockets while his gas tank is filling.

I run my hands up and down his arms. "You should've woke me up."

"You looked peaceful." He leans in for a kiss. His lips are cold. Soon they turn warm.

I miss him already, and he's standing here with his lips pressed to mine.

I don't want to think about tomorrow. There is no tomorrow. Just a nightmare—a nightmare starring me, the dipshit who stole a baby.

I can't close my eyes. I have to see that he's real. That at one time I had this wonderful guy who loved me. I have to remember this. I have to etch it into my skull.

The loud *thunk* of the gas nozzle shutting off brings us back to where we are—standing under a brightly lit gas station awning.

"Go ahead and get back in." He pulls the nozzle out of the truck, and I scoot back around to my side and jump in.

Addy's restless. I dig in the diaper bag for a pacifier and pop one in her mouth, then cover her with a flannel baby blanket. She gives the pacifier a few sucks, then settles back into a sound sleep.

Chris hops into the cab, starts the truck, and rubs his hands together. I prop my foot up on the dashboard, feeling bitchy. I want to break something.

"We can always turn around. You don't have to go back, you know. If there's trouble, it'll find you anyway and we can deal with it at home." He threads his fingers with mine. His eyes plead.

Home. Home is a white cape cod on Maple Street with dark green awnings over the windows. There's a park down the street, and a grandma who loves Addy.

We should go home.

But there was the cop and the newspaper. I got past those, but I don't know what's waiting around the next corner. I can't let Chris find out the truth that way, from a cop or a journalist, someone other than me.

"I can't." I pound my fist against my leg. "There's no way. I have to do this."

He holds up his hands. "Okay. Okay. I get it." He jerks the truck into gear and takes off out of the gas station and back onto the highway.

This isn't how it should be. He *can't* be mad at me. Not *now*. "I'm not mad at you, you know."

He nods but keeps his eyes straight ahead. His mouth forms a tight line.

"I'm sorry if I upset you." My words make me wince inside. I'm about to crush him.

He takes a deep breath. "No. It's cool." He manages a wobbly smile.

"So. Your dad and Gail . . ." Might as well get him pissed at someone other than me.

He looks at me and rolls his eyes. "Don't worry, I know all about it. Dad had to tell me when I found the cans of paint in the garage last night. He doesn't usually use every primary color the hardware store sells. The room is going to be obnoxious. Guess it fits Jonathan, though."

"You're okay with it?"

He lets out a chuckle. "What do I care? I'm not going to be there to see it, am I?"

I might be having an out-of-body experience, because I detest myself so much, I'm trying to leave myself behind. I hate myself more than Mom could ever hate me.

I came into his life, wrecked it, and now I'm planning to ditch him six hours away from home.

A home he doesn't even belong in anymore.

A home that's already moved on without him.

He rubs my thigh. "Have you talked to your mom? Does she know I'm coming home with you? I'll stay in a hotel until I can find a place."

"Yeah, she's cool with it."

Hate. Hate. Hate. Me. Me. Me.

"I figured when you didn't say anything that it was cool." He glances over. "Think we should stop somewhere overnight instead of driving straight through?"

"No. Let's just get there. I'll drive if you get tired." I have a freaking flight to catch, and another night with him would kill me. I already mentally prepared myself to never see him again, no matter how much it will tear me apart. No matter how much it will tear him apart.

I sit on my hands and clutch the leather seat. Through the dashboard, headlights barrel past us, leaving trails of blurry white light behind. What kind of trail will I leave behind? I glance at Chris out of the corner of my eye, then back out the window again.

At 1:00 a.m., Addy's awake and hungry. We've just passed the welcome sign to the small town outside Atlanta that I'd pointed out on Chris's map. My plan is coming together.

Chris pulls into an IHOP parking lot. "I'm starving. How about you? Can you go for some pancakes?"

I'll puke all over him if I eat. "Sure!"

I dawdle getting out of the truck. He has to get out first so I can "forget" the diaper bag without him remembering and picking it up. I adjust my shorts in the parking lot before pushing the passenger seat forward and reaching into the back for Addy. I fumble with her seat belt.

"Need some help?" Chris asks from behind me.

"No, I'm good. It's just twisted. Go ahead. I'm coming."

"I'll wait while you get her out. I'm not leaving you in the parking lot by yourself at night." His hand rests on my lower back.

A lump forms in my throat at his touch, making it hard to swallow.

A single thought streaks through my mind: *It's almost over.*

Instead of forgetting the diaper bag, which I know will never work with him standing there, I tip it over, making it look like an accident and spilling its contents all over the back floor of his truck. "Shit!"

"What's wrong?" His hand rubs across my back.

"I just spilled everything out of the diaper bag."

He yawns. "Oh, well, we're not in a hurry, are we?"

"No."

Quickly, I gather all of Addy's supplies back in the bag but shove the can of powdered formula under the seat. Then I whisk Addy and the bag into my arms and out of the truck.

We walk side by side into IHOP and follow the hostess to a booth in the back. The overhead lights hurt my eyes— everything is blindingly bright compared with the darkness of the truck for the past six hours. My face and hair feel greasy even though I showered before we left. Something about traveling makes me look and feel like shit.

A server comes by for our drink orders. When she leaves the table, Chris excuses himself to go to the men's room. Knowing this is probably my only opportunity, I find the number for the airport shuttle and scurry to the pay phone with Addy.

My shaky fingers plunk the coins into the phone and press the numbers. Every few seconds, I look over my shoulder to make sure he's not standing behind me.

"Shuttle service," a rushed male voice answers on the other side of the phone line.

"Hi," I say in a low, quiet voice, "I need a lift to the airport. I'm at IHOP—"

"I'm sorry, ma'am, we're not a taxi service. We only pick up from the airport hotels. You'll need to call a cab." And he hangs up.

My stomach lurches as I replace the receiver. I'm screwed.

Addy starts squirming and squawking, ready to stir up a storm. I haul her into the ladies' room and change her two-ton, soggy diaper. She'll need to eat soon, but she'll just have to wait until we're on the plane—if I can think of a way to get us there.

Back out in the booth, Chris is sitting, playing with his keys.

I sit down across from him and scan his face, committing it to memory before I do what I know will seal my fate with him forever, and say, "I can't find Addy's formula. It must be out in the truck." I hold out my hand for him to entrust me with his keys.

He hesitates, but before he can offer to get the formula himself, I add, "I want to change her out there too. The ladies' room is disgusting!" The keys dangle above my palm, and I reach up and snatch them out of his grasp. "Be right back."

Those are my last words to him.

Be right back.

Another lie uttered on my way to the parking lot, where I'll steal his truck.

My vision is spinning as I walk to the doors and push them open. Don'tcrydon'tcrydon'tcry.

Being strong is my only option at this point.

Tears won't help me drive away.

With Addy buckled in, I scrawl one final sentence on the outside of my finished, twelve-page letter to Chris:

Pick up your truck at the airport.

After tucking the letter inside the mesh compartment on the end of his duffel bag, where he'll be sure to see it, I toss the bag onto the IHOP sidewalk and drive away.

chapter

twenty-
four

I've never been this upset. I'm screaming and sobbing, banging my fists on the steering wheel. My stomach burns. I jerk the wheel to the side of the road, throw the door open, and puke.

It's in my hair, and I couldn't care less. I remember the first day with Chris, when he wiped Addy's spit-up from my hair with a paper towel. She's in the back of the truck shrieking. I've completely freaked her out.

I wipe my face and mouth on my sleeve, get back behind the wheel, and slam the door shut.

I can't fall apart now.

I have a plane to catch.

One hour and forty minutes after boarding, the plane pulls up to the gate at Akron-Canton Airport.

I'm home, and it's the last place on earth I want to be.

Fed and sleeping, Addy's cradled in my arm. I lug our bags along with my other hand.

Out on the sidewalk, the night air's thick. It's humid and muggy. Mosquitoes buzz around my head. The taxi driver takes my bag and asks, "Where to?"

A sense of dread washes over me as I give him Mom's address.

Addy sighs into my neck as I settle into the back of the taxi. Her breath's warm and dry, and it smells sweet. I kiss the side of her head, weariness easing its way through my limbs.

It's 4:15 a.m. Mom won't be awake. The spare key will be under the doormat like always. I'll just sleep in my room with Addy, in my old bed, and confront Mom when she wakes up.

The taxi comes to a stop, jerking me out of the daze I was in, with my head dropped back against the seat. Out of the window, my old house comes into focus. Even through the darkness, I can tell that in the months I've been gone, the house has fallen apart even more.

"You sure this is the right address?" the driver asks, peering back at me and Addy.

I nod. "Unfortunately, it is." I hand him his money and tug on the door handle.

The driver goes around to the trunk and takes out our bags. "Do you need help with your bags?"

"I can manage. Thanks." I sling the bags over my shoulder and carry Addy through the high grass to the front stoop. My hand finds the key under the mat, and I try to stick it in the lock.

But it won't work.

I shove, attempting to force it in.

It's not the key for this lock.

Mom changed the locks. Hope and I are gone, and she wants to make sure we stay that way.

"Everything okay?" the driver shouts.

I wave. "It's cool." The words stab my stomach.

Shit. I have to knock.

The taxi's gone, so I hope she answers. I reluctantly pound on the door, loud enough to wake a drugged-up, drunk old woman. After a minute, I pound again.

Inside, footsteps thud into the family room.

The lock clicks.

The door is flung open.

I didn't think it was possible, but Mom looks worse than she did when I left. There's no way she's showered in the past week, and her hazy eyes scream, *Binge!*

"Hell do you want?" she slurs. Her feet stagger to the left, and she almost falls, but she catches herself on the doorjamb.

"I brought the baby back. I know it was wrong. I understand I'm screwed. Hugely."

I won't say I'm sorry. I'm not.

She laughs, bitterly. "Didn't like playing momma? Sucks ass, doesn't it?" She sways against the door but steadies herself again. Her face hardens. "Get the hell out of here! I never want to see you again!"

Her hand rises to strike. I curl in on myself to protect Addy. "I'm going! I'll drop the baby off at Dave and Angel's, okay?"

More cold laughter. "Angel left Dave, and he bailed. He's been gone for months. Nobody wants that damn kid."

I can only imagine the look on my face that prompts her wicked, wholly satisfied grin. "Looks like you've got yourself a baby and no place to live. Guess you should go back to wherever you came from." She takes a few measured steps backward before slamming the door in my face and locking it.

No kidnapping charges.
No auto theft charges.
No teen jail.
No Angel and Dave.
No home.
No Hope.
No Chris.
The no's could go on for days.
But there is Addy. She's asleep in the center of a hotel bed, the same way we started this mess.

I get to keep her. She's mine for real now. Nobody else wants her.

Go back to wherever you came from, Mom said. Yeah. Like I can. I screwed that up too. I should've just called Mom from Florida when I called Hope. I could've stayed.

I'd be sleeping beside Chris right now.

Addy would be in her Pack 'n Play, curled up in a ball under her blanket.

I don't know how this all went so wrong. Maybe it was my warped intentions in the beginning. Saving Addy was an afterthought. I set out to hurt Mom. I savored every moment of making her life hell while she was pregnant. I knew taking the baby and leaving Mom without that big payout would be a stake to her heart.

This is my big payout—homeless with a three-month-old baby and a couple hundred bucks to my name.

There are times when I look at Addy and I can see her at my age. Her hair will be long and dark, flowing down her back, her eyes will reveal experience beyond her years—how could they not, with a teen mom?

That's what I am to her. I'm Mom. I was never a sister.

I hover over her on the bed. She rubs her eyes with her fists. Her mouth opens and closes like a fish.

When will I tell her the truth? When she's ten? Twelve?

Never. I'll never tell her that nobody wanted her but me.

I lie beside her. Her eyelids flutter open, and she reaches for my face. I let her smack my cheek and laugh. I laugh with her.

"We'll be okay." I hold her wrist. Her bones are bird thin. "We figured it out the first time it was just the two of us. We'll figure it out again."

Hotels won't be as bad now that she sleeps through the night. I just need to get my hands on more money.

I need Hope.

After our phone call, I'm not sure what she'll do when I show up. She doesn't want me around her. The *other* Faith, sure. *This* Faith, the babynapping Faith, not so much.

She'll have to get over it, though. I have Addy to take care of, and she's more important than my pride or Hope's shiny new life.

Our bus to Columbus leaves in twenty minutes. In a little over two hours, we'll be spending our Saturday afternoon searching all over the Ohio State campus for Hope. Our odds of finding her are slim. The only thing that might save me is Hope being on the track team. Someone might know her, or where the team hangs out.

Calling her first won't happen. I won't repeat the last phone conversation we had. College has changed Hope. Like me, she's been itching to get out from under the past eighteen years of her life. I just hadn't realized that meant away from me, too. I don't know if things would be different if I hadn't taken Addy. Something tells me she would be just as over me anyway.

It's 432 steps to the bus stop. I'm gasping for air when I get there. Even though it wasn't that far, holding a baby and two heavy bags makes it a long walk.

I wait on the bench and think about Chris. My mind plays through all of his possible reactions to finding me and Addy gone and only my letter left behind in his bag on the sidewalk.

God, I can picture him pushing through the door of the IHOP into the dark night dotted by the parking lot lights. He'd stop and stare, confused by the empty spot where he'd left his truck parked.

What would he think? How long would it take him to realize I'd left him and wasn't coming back? Did he call his dad and ask for a ride home? He must've been so humiliated, so hurt.

He'd cry into his Spiderman pillow, punching his mattress and raging against another loss—two losses—he didn't deserve. He'd fight himself to not go upstairs and sleep in my bed where the two of us had spent every night for the past couple of months.

How could he stand to see the empty space where Addy had slept in her Pack 'n Play? Where she rolled over for the first time? How could he bear to remember the way she smiled and laughed when he held her beside the window, talking about the squirrels outside?

I pinch the skin on my forearm to relocate the pain from my chest. A physical pain I can handle, more than the endless urge to lie down and die. It's times like these, when Addy's quiet and content, that I need a way to get out of my own head and stop thinking about what I've done to Chris.

For the second time in his life, he's lost two people in an instant. Just . . . gone. No warning.

Addy is sitting on my lap, leaning back against me, sucking on her fist. Every now and then she bounces and makes a sound like "uhn."

If Hope can't help us, or doesn't want to help us, I have to decide if keeping Addy is the best thing to do. There have to be a lot of people looking for babies like her. She could have a perfect home somewhere with a mom and dad who love her, who will put her in a pink room with little white furniture and a dollhouse in the corner.

That's what I've wanted for her even before she was born. A swing set, a baby pool, a sandbox, a doting mom and dad, and a safe neighborhood to play in.

I twist the hair on her head around my finger. I can't give her those things. Not anymore.

I alternate between dozing and crying on the bus ride. There's an old man in front of us. When we got on, he turned around and said, "I hope that baby doesn't cry the whole way." But I'm the one who cries, not Addy.

The bus stops at the terminal in Columbus, and the old man stands up to get off. He looks over the seat to where I'm sitting, holding Addy. "You have a content baby. You know what that means, don't you?"

I roll my eyes. I don't need this right now.

"It means you're a good mom. Not many young mothers are. It's a big responsibility." He smiles and steps out into the aisle.

Whatever. I'm so great at this that I don't even know where

we're sleeping tonight. But call me Mom of the Year.

Crazy old man.

I get us off the bus and onto another, one that will take us to campus. My nerves can't be more shot than they already are, so I don't feel anything when I think about seeing Hope. Even though her help is a long shot, she's my only chance at keeping Addy.

chapter

twenty- five

When I finally find the track, I don't need to be close to know which one she is. Hope's long, golden ponytail flies out behind her as she sprints toward the next hurdle. Her long, tan legs whip out—one straight in front, one bent behind—as she leaps over it.

All of a sudden, I realize I have no business being here. I'm an intruder in Hope's life now. After practices, she plants her fancy track shoes, paid for with student grant money, at the base of her bed, in her dorm room, where the air is fresh and clean, free of stale cigarette smoke and beer stench.

My feet freeze to the ground just inside the field. I can't take one more step.

She really did get free.

I twist around, the treads of my sneakers yanking up dirt and grass. This was a mistake. My feet come off the ground and allow me to take a few strides.

"Faith?" Hope's voice crashes into me from behind.

I turn to find her jogging toward me.

"What are you doing here?"

Her face is flushed, windburned.

I muster a stunted smile. "I'm not sure. Didn't know what else to do." Then the tears start. They stream down like a faucet has been turned on full blast inside my skull.

She's a blur, but I feel her squeeze my arm. "Hang on. Stay right here." Then she leaves me standing there looking like an idiot seventeen-year-old with a baby who's been kicked in the ass by life. And that's exactly what I am.

Hope's dorm room is just how I pictured it, cold from the AC, neat and clean, and smelling of nothing at all.

I'm instantly jealous. She hands me a bottle of water and plops down on her bed next to me, eyeing Addy. "Why?"

I lean back against her wall and shrug. "At first, I just wanted to punish Mom. She wouldn't get the money without the baby. Then I wanted to get Addy out of there so she didn't end up like us."

"Addy? That's her name?"

I raise an eyebrow. "Something wrong with her name?"

"No. I guess I just didn't think that you would name her."

I laugh. I can't help it. "You didn't think I'd name a baby I've had for almost three months? Good thing you got a track scholarship, brainiac."

She shoves my leg. "Shut up."

We're quiet for a minute. Then she says, "Mom doesn't want her." It's not a question. It never has been. "Dave's gone."

"I know."

"What are you going to do? Where have you been living all this time?"

"With friends."

"Are you going back?"

I shake my head. "Can't."

She nods like she's not surprised to hear I can't go back, that I screwed it up.

"You can't stay here." She looks around the shoebox-size room she shares with a roommate.

"No shit."

"What do you want, then?"

"Money." The word feels like poison shooting off my tongue. When you've never had it, asking for money is like asking for a person's soul.

She stands up and moves across the room.

Poison.

"I don't have any." She turns to her desk.

"You have to have something." I can't stand pressing her, but I know she got grant money, and if there's even a little bit left, I could keep Addy for another day or two.

Hope spins back around. "I'm here on a scholarship and grants. Why would I have money?"

"Brian does." The words are out before I have a chance to stop them. Desperation has taken over the filter between my brain and mouth.

She purses her lips and shakes her head, looking at the ceiling. "I'm supposed to drag him into your mess too, huh?"

Why can't she see what even twenty bucks would do for me? "Just forget it." I stand and start for the door. "We'll just starve and sleep on the street. Have a nice life. Try not to feel too guilty tonight sleeping in your bed."

Her hand slams down on the desk. "Fine! Just wait outside and let me call him. Give me two freakin' minutes, Faith, okay?"

I nod and leave her room to wait out in the hallway. I shut the door behind me. It echoes in the empty hall. Nobody's around. Addy's heavy in my arm, so I lean against the wall and switch her to the other side.

Then my breath catches—someone's strumming a guitar.

I know with every ounce of my being that I'll never be able to hear a guitar again without my heart squeezing, threatening to stop.

Hope doesn't come out of her room, but fifteen minutes later, Brian shows up and hands me an envelope.

"Thanks," I whisper, unable to meet his eyes.

He pats Addy's head. "She looks a little like Hope."

"Yeah, she does."

He knocks on the door. "Hey, it's me."

She opens it. Her face is red and puffy from crying. "I'm sorry I had to ask—"

"Don't worry about it." His hands cup her chin.

I can still feel Chris's hands on my face.

"Did you tell him thank you, at least?" she asks me.

"She did," he says.

"Hope, I . . ." I don't know what to say to her. "Thanks. We'll leave you alone."

She lets Brian slide past her and inside the room. "Where are you going to go?"

I shake my head. "I don't know."

She bites the inside of her cheek. "Stay close. I want to know you're okay." Then she lunges for me and wraps her arms around me, squishing Addy between us.

"I thought you were done with your past . . . with me."

She lets me go. "I am done with my past, but you're my Faithy." She wipes her eyes, pushes my hair up, and leans in to kiss the back of my neck, right on my tattoo—the twin to her own. "Call me and let me know where you are."

"Okay."

I leave, feeling like Addy and I aren't completely alone in the world after all.

Brian's envelope holds five hundred dollars. The first thing I do is hit the McDonald's right off campus. I haven't eaten in a day and a half.

Addy's propped in a high chair with Ronald McDonald's face on the back of the seat. I stuffed a blanket around her so she wouldn't slide down or tip to the side. She's watching me eat like she'd pounce on my burger if she could.

"Want a fry?" I hand her one. Screw the books, she can gnaw on a fry for a while. What can it hurt? Maybe we'll skip the rice cereal and baby food I'm supposed to give her soon and go right to fast food. She seems to like it.

She's mine, anyway. I'm making the rules now.

She coughs and I grab her. She stuffed the entire fry into her mouth. I swipe my finger over her tongue and fish it out. My eyes stay on her face, making sure she doesn't have a piece of fry stuck in her throat and doesn't turn blue. Older, more responsible people wouldn't have done that. She should be with somebody who knows what they're doing.

"Is she okay?" I turn around to see the middle-aged woman in the booth behind me watching us. Her husband's reading the newspaper, oblivious.

"I think so. Yeah."

"Don't feel bad. I did the same thing when my youngest was about her age. God makes them resilient so they can endure our learning curve." She laughs. "Both of mine are in college now. Enjoy her. Before you know it, she'll be out of the house." She gives Addy a wave and turns back around.

Learning curve? How can I be sure I'll come out of the curve? I might crash right into the guardrail with Addy riding shotgun.

Good thing God makes them resilient. If you say so, lady.

I give Addy a bottle and change her diaper before we leave. There's a bus stop right outside. We wait there, and the bus comes within a half hour. I ask the driver to stop at the nearest hotel that won't cost me a fortune.

In the last seat on the bus, I sit and break down.

I can't do this.

I don't know how.

The next day, we wake in our hotel room and go through our routine: bottle, bath, diaper, fresh clothes. I call Hope and tell her where we are. Then I spend my time trying not to think about the ultimate decision that looms in the corner of the room.

For no reason at all, I flip through the phone book to the government agencies.

Social Services.

I stare at the number until it turns to nothing but dots in front of my eyes.

Then I slam the phone book shut and drop my head down on top of it.

Addy's on the floor rolling around, trying to lift her head and chest off the floor. She slides her knees underneath her and shoves, then her arms give out and she falls on her chest. Her face shows determination in her creased brow and focused eyes. She won't give up.

Maybe she doesn't need to be resilient. She's tough. Maybe even tough enough to survive me.

But she can't survive starvation, and I don't have much

money. When what Brian gave me is gone, we're screwed. I can't ask him again—there's no way.

My decision will be made for me.

I sit up and clutch the phone book to my chest and close my eyes.

This is going to hurt.

chapter

twenty-
six

Mrs. Wilkins is our social worker. "You're living here in this room?" she asks, with her creased, plum-colored suit and black flats. Her hair is short and sticks to her head.

"Yes." I look around. "Not permanently or anything." What's her deal? It's clean. The maid comes every day. It's an assload better than where I grew up.

Her eyes stay on Addy for a few minutes. She doesn't say anything, just watches her as she rolls around again. After two days, she hasn't scooted an inch, but she's still not giving up.

"She seems well-adjusted."

Is she waiting for me to respond or something? "Uh, thanks?"

"Has she been to all of her well visits? Are her shots up to date?"

"No." I bite my lips.

She jots down something in her notebook, probably that I suck.

"Has she had any shots at all?"

I shrug. "Just what they gave her in the hospital."

"Do you have her birth certificate here with you?"

"No."

"Well, we'll need that to proceed. She can't be placed without it."

"What if I can't get it?"

"The county keeps a record. You'll just have to stop and get a copy."

"What if my name's not on her birth certificate?" I cringe, waiting for her to pull her cell phone out and call 911 to report a kidnapping. "She's my mom's baby—my sister. My mom doesn't want her."

Her eyebrows shoot to the ceiling and she blinks double time. "How old are you?"

I lie—fast—without hesitation. "Nineteen." She's not taking Addy this second, like I know she will if she finds out I'm underage.

"And you're her legal guardian?"

"Not yet. This was pretty sudden."

She closes her notebook. "Okay. When you have legal guardianship, we can proceed. Until then, try to get her health record up to date."

She shakes my hand, and I walk her to the door. "I'll check back with you," she says. I watch her walk down the sidewalk, her shoes clicking against the concrete.

"I can't even give you away," I say to Addy. I sigh. "Legal guardianship. Perfect."

There's no way I'm getting Mom involved with Addy again. I want her just where she is—out of Addy's life. It's shocking that she hasn't thought of selling Addy to some black-market adoption gang.

Maybe I'll just put an ad in the paper and find a good home for Addy myself. Maybe they won't care if she doesn't come with all the right paperwork. Maybe they'll even let me visit her.

I shudder with the realization that I'm thinking like a pet owner with a litter of puppies to give away.

I stride over to Addy and scoop her up. I love the weight of her in my arms, and the smell of her new-baby skin, even her spitty fingers poking my cheeks.

Who will I be without her?

Who will I have?

Nobody.

It can't be about me, though. I have to put her first. Living in a hotel room for a few more days and then who knows where—probably on the street—isn't how I want her to be raised.

I took her in the first place so she could have a better life. We just got lucky. We found Ivy.

We found Chris.

But that's over for us, and I don't have anything to offer her anymore. Just love, and you can't eat love for dinner. Ketchup packets aren't so great either.

The answer floods my brain like a flame flickering to life. I know exactly how to do this without the paperwork and red tape, even if I don't want to, even if it's going to kill me to hand her over to someone else.

We walk to the library, where I know there will be a computer I can use. Inside, it smells like dusty old books. It's one of my favorite smells. It's comforting, which is what I need right now.

With Addy on my lap, I type a classified to post online:

Homeless baby needs adoptive parents. Baby left at church. If you can give her a good home, please call.

After I type the phone number to our hotel room, I post it as fast as I can before I have time to think about it.

chapter

twenty-
seven

The next day, I start to panic. The phone hasn't rung.

I don't really want it to.

But it has to. I'm out of money. I would've never guessed diapers and formula were so expensive and that babies needed so much of both. I try to eat minimally, spending only a buck or two on fast food.

Addy's lying on the floor watching *Sesame Street* and being still for once.

Eating a cheeseburger every other day isn't giving me enough energy to keep up with her. I'm light-headed and ready to fall over at any second. All I want is a nap. Or even a shower, but I can't watch her and take a shower at the same time, so I have to wait until she finally goes to sleep. Now that she's rolling around, I have to worry all night long that she's going to wake up and fall off the bed.

My mom was right, being a mom kind of does suck sometimes.

Just as Addy goes to reach for the lamp cord beside the bed, the phone rings. I'm sure it's not as loud as it seems, but my ears buzz as the sound reverberates inside them.

I lunge off the bed and grab Addy.

This is it.

I can feel it.

"Hello?" I hold my breath.

"Hello. My wife and I saw the ad online about the baby. She's on the line too—my wife. We'd like to talk to you and maybe set up a time to meet."

I talk to Mr. and Mrs. Schroeder for an hour. He's a teacher. She's a lawyer. They live close, in a first-rate school district, in a big house, in a nice neighborhood. They attend church, have tried any and all methods of getting pregnant, and have recently begun looking into adoption, which is how they ended up finding my ad from an Internet search.

We arrange a meeting the next day at noon, at a restaurant around the corner. If it ends up that they're not serial killers in disguise, I'll go to their house and they'll show me Addy's room. They've had a nursery ready for three years.

Just add baby.

Just add Add.

Just delete me.

I think I've washed my hair five times, but my mind isn't in the shower with me, it's cycling through my conversation with the Schroeders over and over. How can I hand her over tomorrow to people I don't even know?

My hand grips the faucet and turns off the water. I'm on

autopilot. Feet step out. Hand grabs towel. This is how I'll live for the rest of my life.

Numb.

If I could just get my mind to shut down like my emotions have, I'd be set. But it won't. Right now, it's picturing me back at school next month. My senior year. There's no way I can go back there. I just don't fit in anymore.

I don't fit anywhere.

I used to fit with Chris.

I still ache for him.

So much for being numb and emotionless.

I make my hands tug a T-shirt over my head and yank underwear up my legs. My feet walk me over to the bed, and I crawl in next to Addy.

This could be our last night together. I'm not sure. Will they want to keep her tomorrow?

I pull her close. She fits against my stomach, a little comma-shaped pillow of baby for me to cuddle with. She lets out her sigh and gurgle and starts moving her mouth around like she's carrying on a dream conversation. I wish I knew what she was saying. I wish I was going to be around for her first word.

I wake crying. Morning wasn't supposed to come this fast.

Addy's happy. She's making little humming, yelling, almost singing noises, and kicking her feet in the air. I wonder if she knows she's hitting the jackpot today.

I can't lift my head off the pillow. There are too many heavy thoughts weighing it down. After I hand her over and they take her away . . . then what? Where do I go? With all my attention focused on keeping Addy fed and making sure we have a place to sleep, I haven't had to think about myself. She was my driving force. When she's gone, what happens to me?

I just want to pull the covers over my head and cry all day. Maybe I should just have them come and take her to get it over with. Then I'll lie here, comatose, until the hotel kicks me out.

Addy doesn't like my plan. She wants a bottle. I shuffle over to the minifridge and pull out her second-to-last one. "Guess this really is it, Add. They can buy formula and even baby food. You're going to be their princess."

After I give her the bottle and bathe her, I dig through her clothes, looking for the best of Emma's hand-me-downs. There's a pink dress with a butterfly on it that has matching leggings. "I think this is the one," I tell her. "Your new mommy will love you in this." My voice cracks, and I swallow hard.

She kicks while I pull on her leggings, and squirms when I tug the dress over her head. Then I crash back down on the bed and let her roll around on the floor, making her last few passes over the hotel carpet.

I feel like a turnstile with everyone in my life shoving past, leaving me spinning in circles. I hardly have time to recover before someone else speeds through. I can't take it anymore.

I don't want to live like this.

I'm so hungry. I'm trembling with the effort of getting out of bed. It takes all my strength to pull on jeans and brush my hair and teeth. I don't need to look perfect. It's not me they're adopting.

Addy lies beside me as I stuff my clothes into my duffel bag. Hers I leave separate. They're not coming with mine anymore.

Saying good-bye this time isn't something I can wrap my head around. Before, when I thought she was going with Angel and Dave, there was a slight chance I'd see her again.

This time, good-bye is for keeps. I won't ever see her again.

She pats my leg with her chubby hand. Then she lays her head on my calf.

"Are you tired, baby?" Just before taking her in my arms, I anticipate the feel of her little body. I have to make sure I've got it right and commit it to memory.

I hold her against me and lean back against the dresser. If I close my eyes and squeeze her tight enough, maybe I can wish us out of this mess.

This might be an out-of-body experience. I'm honestly no longer inside my own head. It's like watching myself from someone else's eyes.

Faith swings Addy's diaper bag over her shoulder.

Faith takes one last look around the room she's lived in for the past week with the baby she'll never see again.

Faith hears a knock on the door and stares at it like it's playing a cruel joke. Nobody's out there. She's hearing things.

Two steps forward brings Faith to the door. She leans against it and peers out the peephole.

He stares back at the peephole with his blue-green eyes.

I slam back inside my head. Maybe I imagined the knock. My heart races, until I remember nobody's after me. Nobody cares enough about me or Addy to send the cops after us. We're not wanted—by the police or anybody else.

But I would swear I saw his blue-green eyes through the peephole.

What if he came to find me—to find *us*?

Addy squeals, breaking my stare at the door. I glance down at her, watching for a few seconds, making sure she's real, that this isn't all a dream. I pick her up, then reach out and turn the doorknob, ready to face whatever is on the other side.

acknowledgments

Like the Little Engine That Could, *Leap of Faith* has had a long journey into readers' hands. If it wasn't for a fantastic author and friend, Kathleen Peacock, this novel would be only a manuscript saved in a file on my laptop.

Faith's story had the extraordinarily good fortune to be read by the best agent a writer could ask for, Emmanuelle Morgen, while, coincidentally, Emmanuelle was in Jacksonville, Florida. It was meant to be!

Leap of Faith's editor, Alexandra Cooper, spent so much time and attention to every detail and facet of this story, it wouldn't be what it is without her. Editor Kristin Ostby took over at the finish line with the smooth and graceful transition of a seasoned professional to get *Leap of Faith* released into the wild. I've been very fortunate to work with both of them.

I couldn't imagine a more perfect cover for *Leap of Faith*. Krista Vossen and Shasti O'Leary Soudant surpassed all my wildest dreams.

Annie McElfresh, you are Faith/Leah and Chris's number-one champion. I can't count the number of messages you sent in a year's time, urging me to keep believing in their story. Thank you for that!

Several talented writers have read *Leap of Faith* and given me invaluable feedback and encouragement: Jen Alexander, Rebecca Rogers, Jennifer Wood, Debra Driza, and Kristin

Otts, to name a handful. Also, a big thank-you to everyone who read and cheered me on during Teaser Tuesday snips!

I'd be amiss not to mention the online writers' community on Absolute Write, where several authors gracing the shelves of bookstores learned the ins and outs of the industry. I was fortunate to stumble into the AW Water Cooler and meet a group of women who have been insanely supportive over the years. Cheers, Lit Bitches! You're an amazing group of women.

Lastly, a huge hug and thank-you to my family, who never stopped believing that I could find my way onto the shelves of bookstores. Claudia and Ethan, you are my treasures.